THE FATAL TRIP

Michael Underwood

ST. MARTIN'S
NEW YORK

Printed in Great Britain

Library of Congress Catalog Card Number: 77-76655

First published in the United States of America in 1977

Library of Congress Cataloging in Publication Data

Underwood, Michael, 1916–
    The fatal trip.

    I. Title.
PZ4.E94Fat3   [PR6055.V3]   823'.9'14   77-76655
ISBN 0-312-28507-8

CHAPTER ONE

She felt as if she were watching something in slow motion.

She had arrived late, in time to catch sight of Nick hurrying back into Court. He had obviously been waiting for her outside and then given up. She ran across the marble hall and went to push through the swing doors when a police officer stepped out of the shadows.

'Yes, madam?' His tone had the polite wariness of one who'd had years of experience in dealing with members of the public.

'I'm Detective Sergeant Attwell's wife,' Clare said breathlessly, at the same time pointing at Nick's back which she could see through the glass panel of the inner door.

'A-ah! He's been out looking for you.'

Nick turned as she entered, his expression a mixture of frustration and relief.

'I'm terribly sorry, Nick, but my train was stuck in a tunnel for half an hour . . .'

He gave a perfunctory nod, clearly unwilling to listen to explanations or even to offer a sympathetic cluck for what had been a disagreeable experience.

'The jury's just back,' he hissed, guiding her quickly to a seat and returning to his own place.

It was the first time that Clare had been in one of the Old Bailey's new courts and her first reaction was that if she'd had to pay for her seat, she would have made a fuss at the box office.

Admittedly she had an unobstructed view of the dock and it was, after all, to observe its occupant that Nick had urged her to come. By twisting her neck she could see counsel and half the jury, but the judge was completely out of sight.

It appeared that there was some hitch in bringing the defendant from the cells where he had been awaiting the jury's verdict, but now a door into the dock opened and Clare saw a strained, anxious young man shepherded into Court.

He had fair hair and a pleasant face with a wide mouth and a full lower lip. He was neatly dressed and had a clean-limbed look about him. But what immediately caught Clare's notice was the scar which ran for almost an inch along the cheekbone below his right eye, the result, Nick had told her, of a motor cycling accident four years ago when he had been nineteen. Perhaps because of the nervous strain, it now stood out on his face as if it had been superimposed on the skin.

Clare could hear the Clerk of the Court calling out the jurors' names while the young man in the dock stared at them as though mesmerised. The roll call ended.

'Members of the jury, are you agreed upon your verdict?'

'We are,' the foreman announced, staring furiously at a slip of paper in his hand.

'Do you find Stephen Burley guilty or not guilty of burglary?'

'Guilty.'

At one and the same moment, there was a small cry from the public gallery above Clare's head and a thud as the defendant dropped to the floor in a faint.

The two prison officers in the dock, who had been taken completely by surprise, heaved him on to a chair and forced some water past his lips.

From somewhere out of Clare's sight, a voice said, 'The Court will adjourn for a few minutes.' It was a calm, judicial voice, schooled to be unmoved by scenes in Court.

After the judge had retired, Clare continued staring at the slumped figure in the dock, though all she could see was the top of his head and his shoulders. But a few seconds later he was able to stand and, supported at either elbow, he was assisted from Court.

It was at this point that Clare felt as if she had been witnessing something in slow motion.

Nick came across to where she was sitting. He was shaking his head in a worried manner.

'Well, what did you make of that?' he asked in a hollow voice.

Well, what had she made of it? To begin with she was not

6

ready to pronounce *her* verdict so soon, even though the reason for her visit to the Old Bailey, entailing as it had a re-arrangement of domestic routine including the parking of Simon on a good-natured neighbour and then a traumatic journey by tube, was to answer this very question. Or rather, to form an objective, if necessarily superficial, view of Stephen Burley himself.

It was only late in the day, indeed, after the commencement of the trial, that Nick had begun to have doubts about the guilt of the young man he had charged with burglary some weeks earlier. The evidence had all been there, even though the case had depended largely on identification by a single witness. But what an impressive and unshakable witness Eva Sharman had proved to be, Nick had told her. No one could doubt her word – and certainly the jury had not done so.

But Nick's worm of doubt, which had nothing to do with Eva Sharman's truthfulness as a witness, had gnawed so effectively that the previous evening he had urged Clare to drop everything and come to Court next morning.

'I don't know what help I can be,' she had told him. 'Just looking at him sitting in the dock won't tell me much.'

'I want you to come anyway,' Nick had replied. 'If you tell me afterwards you thought he had guilt written all over his face, it'll set my doubts at rest. I'll know that I was becoming fixated.' In an almost pleading tone, he had added, 'I've already told you everything about the case . . .'

Nick always had discussed his cases with her. Having been in the force herself before marrying him, she had a professional interest in his work above and beyond that of a normal loving wife. At the time of her resignation, there had even been one or two senior officers who had voiced the opinion privately that the Metropolitan force was losing the brighter of the two.

And now here she was with Nick standing anxiously over her, being asked to give her own verdict, based not on evidence, but on three minutes' dramatic observation.

'He must have realised there was a fair chance of his being convicted,' Clare stalled.

Nick gave a small helpless shrug. 'I don't know. Anyway,

it still didn't prevent him fainting – and that was genuine enough.'

'Even the guilty have been known to faint when convicted,' she said tentatively.

'I daresay, but all I know is that Burley's faint has made me even more worried. Supposing he *is* innocent, Clare?'

A year ago Nick would have taken the robust attitude that, if the jury decided someone was guilty, it was not for Detective Sergeant Nick Attwell to agonise over the verdict. He was but a small cog in the administration of justice machine and, as long as he played his own role with integrity, he didn't have to concern himself with the responsibilities of others who were part of the same machine.

But that was all before he had himself become the subject of a false accusation and had been suspended from duty for several weeks. Although he had subsequently been vindicated and reinstated, Clare knew that he had been as mentally scarred by the experience as Stephen Burley had been physically scarred by his accident. It was reflected in his attitude toward his cases. He had become more introspective and less sure. Not that he had had any doubts about charging Burley with burglary. It was a straightforward case and one about which the lawyers had never voiced any qualms. Though with identification as the main issue there was always an element of chance.

Clare was still not clear how Nick's doubts had started. All Nick himself could say was that the nearer the case came to its end, the more he had thought about it. Clare surmised that recent public interest in cases involving identity had caused him to brood on the issue in Burley's case. And now the Court of Appeal had issued guidelines to trial judges in such cases in order that so-called unsafe convictions could be avoided.

The result was that its projection as an issue of considerable public interest coincided with Nick's case against Stephen Burley.

As all this passed through Clare's mind, she was prompted to ask about the judge's summing up.

'Prosecuting counsel says it was unfaultable,' Nick remarked glumly. 'He told the jury all the right things about identification. Burley doesn't stand a chance on appeal. He let out a heavy sigh and seemed to sag before Clare's eyes. 'That faint clinched it for me. I'm sure he's innocent. What are we going to do about it, Clare?'

Clare, to her relief, was saved having to give an answer by the judge's return to Court.

Soon afterwards, Burley was brought back into the dock, looking even more pale and taut than earlier. The judge quickly instructed that he should be seated. Clare noticed him give an anguished look up at the public gallery, where she presumed his fiancée must be sitting. It was obviously she who had let out the cry when the verdict was announced.

Prosecuting counsel stood up and informed the judge that he would call Detective Sergeant Attwell to give evidence of the defendant's antecedents.

While Nick made his way across the Court to the witness box, Clare let her gaze run along the row of seats reserved for witnesses who had given evidence.

From Nick's description, she had no difficulty identifying Eva Sharman and Miles Rickard, who had been Burley's employer. They were sitting together at the end of a row, Miss Sharman a picture of almost prim respectability in the sort of hat Clare remembered an elderly aunt wearing on formal occasions. It was dark blue straw and had a very artificial-looking rose pinned to one side. Miles Rickard had a weary, withdrawn appearance and Clare wondered why he had remained to the bitter end. Perhaps he felt that, as employer and owner of the company which had been burgled, duty required him to be there. Clare knew from what Nick had told her that Eva Sharman had been with the company since Miles' father had founded it immediately after the war. She was now sixty-two, but showed no inclination to retire. She had become that familiar figure, the managing director's indispensable personal assistant. She had known Miles since he was a schoolboy and had transferred her loyalty from father to son when Miles stepped into the managing director's shoes on his father's sudden death. Miles himself was now forty-three and twice married.

All this and more Nick had told her, as if every detail of the lives of the participants had to be fed into her personal computer to enable her to give him her assessment. And if when the time came she was unable to remove his doubts, perhaps because she even shared them, what was she going to suggest? It would be no good telling Nick there was nothing he could do and it now rested with others; Appeal Courts and petitions to the Home Secretary. In his present state of mind, he wouldn't accept that. He would still feel obliged to do something himself despite the discouragement of his superiors whose attitude would be that the police had done their job and the matter was now out of their hands. Who, they would ask, was Detective Sergeant Attwell to start crusading against a jury's verdict of guilty?

Clare leaned forward and twisted her head so that she could see Nick in the witness box.

Copies of the antecedent history of the defendant had been handed to counsel on both sides as well as to the judge. Prosecuting counsel indicated that he had no questions to put to Nick and sat down.

Even to Clare who was still in her twenties, Burley's counsel looked very young. This impression was reinforced by the snowy white wig on his head. It was as new as a wedding hat.

'I have one or two questions to ask the officer, my lord,' he said in a pleasantly unaffected voice.

'Certainly, Mr Chant.'

Defending counsel turned toward Nick. 'The antecedents indicate of course that my client has no previous convictions, but would it be fair to say, Sergeant Attwell, that in the course of your enquiries into his background he has emerged as a young man of exemplary character?'

'It would.'

'And that even his employer, Mr Rickard, found it hard to accept that he could have committed this crime?'

'That's correct.'

'And that he was highly thought of by everyone at Rickard Motor Distributors Limited?'

Before Nick was able to answer, the judge's voice broke in. 'But I observe that he'd only worked there for six months, is that correct?'

'Yes, my lord.'

'Still long enough in my submission, my lord, to form a sound judgment of his character,' Mr Chant remarked energetically.

'Yes, Mr Chant, any more questions?' The judge's tone carried no more than a trace of familiar judicial scepticism.

Defending counsel frowned and pursed his lips. Clare decided that, young though he might be, he was not without spirit. Nick had told her that he had defended capably, save that he had not been able to get anywhere in his cross-examination of Eva Sharman. If anyone could have done so, it would have to have been a counsel of long experience in that difficult art.

'Would it be fair to say, Sergeant Attwell, that, in your dealings with him, my client has behaved in a model fashion?'

Once more before Nick could answer, the judge had intervened. 'A model of what?' he asked in a faintly acerbic tone.

'A model of co-operation,' defending counsel added quickly.

'Yes.'

'Do you really mean that, officer?' This time the tone was unmistakably hostile.

'Yes, my lord. He has been model in the sense that he has given no trouble. In my dealings with him, he has always been polite and obliging.'

Clare had by now edged herself sideways sufficiently far to be able to see the judge. He was staring at Nick as though trying to decide just where to insert the point of a rapier.

'Has he told you what he has done with the money?' He paused and, giving weight to every syllable, added, 'With twenty thousand pounds?'

'No, my lord, because he has always denied committing the crime.'

The judge's gaze swept the Court and came to rest on Burley who was sitting rigid in the dock, 'So his co-operation hasn't extended that far?' he remarked, switching his attention back to Nick.

'No, my lord.'

'All you're really saying, officer, is that the defendant hasn't made a nuisance of himself since his arrest, isn't that the sum of it?'

'You could put it that way, my lord.'

11

'Now that we have that small matter straightened out, Mr Chant, is there anything further you wish to ask the officer?'

'Was he due to get married in the coming months?' defending counsel asked, glancing quickly at the judge as if he expected further interruption.

'Yes.'

'To a most respectable girl?'

'Yes.'

'Mr Chant, do you *really* think that helps me?' the judge enquired with a sigh of judicial long-suffering.

'To the extent, my lord, that it shows what a wholly respectable background my client's life has.'

'I accept, Mr Chant, that up until now your client has never come to the notice of the police and has, so far as anyone knows, led a blameless existence. Now, is there anything further you wish to ask the officer?'

'No, my lord.'

'But you wish to address me in mitigation?'

'If your lordship pleases, though I hope not to take up too much of your lordship's time.'

'The Court's time is yours, Mr Chant,' the judge retorted in a spasm of graciousness.

Clare had listened to a good number of pleas in mitigation during her service as a police officer, sometimes in squirming discomfort, but more often in yawning boredom. All too frequently they sounded like cliché-ridden scripts delivered by third-rate actors. The trouble was, she had long ago decided, that nobody believed in their effectiveness. The trial formula required defending counsel to urge leniency upon a judge who had most probably made up his mind what sentence to impose. Hence the conventional clichés on the one side and the distant look of endurance on the other. Obviously there were exceptions, but they were few and far between. At all events, that was Clare's experience. Nick said that he never listened to them and the only ones which ever caught and held his attention were the startlingly fresh or the abysmally bad.

But as she listened to Mr Chant addressing the judge, Clare decided that he was likely to go a long way in his profession. He not only possessed a pleasing voice, but he revealed a

12

fluent use of English. Clare listened; moreover, she noticed that the judge listened. And true to his hope, he spoke for less than ten minutes.

There was a moment's silence when he sat down. Then the judge said, 'Thank you, Mr Chant. Thank you very much.'

Meanwhile the senior dock officer had motioned Burley to stand and he and his colleagues closed in on either side of the defendant to forestall any repetition of what had happened half an hour earlier.

'Stephen Burley,' the judge began, 'the jury has found you guilty of a very serious crime; of burgling the office of your employer and stealing £20,000, and it is my duty to sentence you on the basis of their verdict.'

There was something in the judge's tone which made Clare feel that he had suddenly decided to adopt a neutral stance. He was not, as judges frequently do, going to identify himself with their verdict. She could only think that Mr Chant's plea in mitigation had struck some chord.

'I take into account your previous good character,' he now went on, 'and everything that your counsel has so eloquently urged on your behalf. But this was a serious crime and it is clear that the jury had no hesitation in accepting Miss Sharman's evidence, as they were entitled to do. In all the circumstances, the least sentence I can pass is one of three years' imprisonment.' He paused and then added as he closed his notebook, 'Perhaps I should say that I was originally minded to pass a considerably heavier sentence, but having listened to your counsel and given what I hope is proper weight to the points he has urged upon me, I think that three years is the right sentence.'

Burley had swayed when he first heard his sentence, but now he walked briskly from the dock unaided by his escort. From the fact that he had not glanced up at the public gallery, Clare deduced that his fiancée was no longer in Court, and Nick confirmed this a moment later as he joined her.

'I sent Ted Baskomb up to have a word with her and take her off for a cup of tea,' he said. 'It's bad enough being sent off to prison, without having your girl-friend's cries ringing in your ears.'

13

As they pushed their way out of Court, Detective Constable Baskomb came across the hall.

'I've left her with Burley's brother,' he said. 'She's having a little cry, but she'll be all right. I told her he could easily have got five or six. What with remission and parole, I told her the wedding cake would hardly have time to get stale.' He made to move on. 'I'll go and collect our bits and pieces in Court.'

As D.C. Baskomb departed, Clare could not help reflecting that there was a time when Nick's own attitude would have mirrored that of his side-kick.

'Well, are you ready to tell me what you think?' Nick asked, breaking in on her thoughts.

'I think,' Clare said slowly, 'that you've got to satisfy yourself about this.'

'Meaning exactly what?'

'Meaning that you've got to find out whether Burley may have been innocent. In effect, it means retracing the steps of your original enquiry. At the moment you have no more than a feeling that injustice has been done. You could be quite wrong, but you'll never know unless you dig back into the case.' She looked up at him and smiled. 'Obviously you're not going to be happy doing nothing, which means you've got to do something. And all you *can* do is sift through the evidence all over again.' She paused. 'I don't suppose that course would receive much official backing?'

'You're darned right it wouldn't. I'd probably be told to lay off and that'd be an order.'

'So you'll have to beaver away in your own time and I can't say that I'm too keen on that.'

'There is a solution. You help me.'

'In what way?' Clare asked, with a faint feeling of dread.

'In the first place you could talk to Eva Sharman. After all, she's the beginning and the end of the case against Burley.'

'And how do I set about doing that?' Though she had foreseen that her suggestion of Nick making further enquiries in order to set his mind at rest was likely to lead to the present situation, she was in no mood of ready acquiescence. She felt herself being drawn inevitably into something she would much sooner stay out of. On the other hand, if it was necessary for

14

Nick's peace of mind, she was prepared to help him in any way she could.

'It wouldn't be difficult to devise a meeting,' Nick said eagerly. 'We can easily think up some ploy.'

'And who looks after Simon while I'm running around on your behalf?' she asked, still fighting off the inevitable.

'My parents would love to have him for a few days. You know they would.'

Clare did, indeed, know this. Also that Simon would return home spoilt and fractious at the imposition of his normal routine.

'If he's to go anywhere, I think it had better be to Molly's.' Molly was Clare's half-sister who lived in Sussex and had three children of her own, but who never seemed to mind having additional ones dumped on her.

'Sure,' Nick said. 'You can call her as soon as you get home.'

They had reached the top of a flight of stairs leading down to the main exit. Clare paused.

'I don't know whether it's good or bad. All I know is that it would be much worse to do nothing. I couldn't live with myself if I thought an innocent person had gone to prison partly as a result of my efforts. Or failure of them.'

'It's not going to be easy, dearest.'

'It'll be less difficult if you help me.'

'And if it ever comes out that I've been running around meddling in one of your cases, you realise that fur will fly in all directions.'

'We'll cope with that if and when it happens.'

'O.K., Sergeant Attwell, if your mind is made up, we'll discuss the next step over supper this evening.'

'Thank you, love,' Nick said with feeling, looking happier than he had done all day.

CHAPTER TWO

On the day after Stephen Burley's conviction, Sharon Pratt forced herself to return to work, though what she really felt like doing was hiding in a dark cave and crying. She had never felt so desolate and deserted in all her life. She had no family in London and very few friends. Ever since she had met Steve, her spare moments had been devoted to him. His parents lived just outside London and had always been nice to her. In fact, their son's downfall had brought them even closer to Sharon in their shared misfortune. But after what had happened in Court yesterday, Mrs Burley had taken to her bed in a state of shock and Mr Burley had withdrawn behind several walls of silence.

During the two years she had been working in London, Sharon had lived in a rented room. She was employed in the typing pool of a government department and, though she found the work of no interest, had decided to remain there until after she and Steve were married.

Apart from her only close friend in the pool, a considerably older girl, she had told no one of what had happened to Steve. She hadn't even told her parents who lived in a Shropshire village and who were never likely to read such small publicity as the case received. She had sustained herself on the certainty of his acquittal. She knew he couldn't have committed such a crime, so how could he ever be found guilty? The shock of his conviction had left her in a state of numbness so that she gazed at the hand which lifted a cup to her lips as if it didn't belong to her.

As she arrived back at the house in which she rented a room after that first hideous day (worse by far than the day on which Steve had been arrested), she noticed a young woman hovering on the pavement outside. She was about to pass by, when the woman smiled at her.

16

'Miss Pratt?'

'Yes.'

'My name's Clare Reynolds. I'm a social worker. I've called to have a word with you about what's happened to your fiancé. I was in Court yesterday.'

When she and Nick had discussed the matter the previous evening, Clare had said quite firmly that she would like to begin her enquiries with Sharon Pratt. This would not only be a much easier interview than one with Eva Sharman, but it would also give her an opportunity of forming her own view of Burley through the eyes of his fiancée. Once this had been agreed, they had decided that Clare should use her maiden name and, for this initial venture, should call herself a social worker, which, in a sense, she was.

'I'm afraid my room's at the top,' Sharon said, accepting the visit without question and leading the way into the house. She didn't speak again until they reached the top landing and she inserted a key into the door of her room. 'It's an awful mess.' It was more a statement of fact than an apology.

There was an unmade bed in one corner and a sink full of unwashed cups and plates in another. On a table in the centre of the room was a rumpled newspaper and a jar of instant coffee with the lid screwed on at a crooked angle.

Picking some clothes off a chair and throwing them on to the bed, she said, 'Would you like to sit here? I'm not very tidy at the best of times, but I'm afraid it's worse than usual.'

'Thats understandable,' Clare replied with a friendly smile. 'The past few weeks must have been a great ordeal.'

'Nothing's been as bad as yesterday. I still don't believe it happened. How can someone be sent to prison for something he's not done? Three years!' Her mouth began to tremble and she turned her head away from Clare. 'If that's so-called British justice, it's just a mockery.' She turned back and met Clare's gaze. 'Steve never did it, Miss Reynolds. I know he didn't.'

She looked like the country girl that Clare knew her to be. She had rosy cheeks and large grey eyes and medium brown hair which fell to her shoulders on either side from a parting in the middle. She had the simple, trusting look about her of many of the young girls who find their way to London. The difference in her case was that the look was still there two years later.

'How do you know?' Clare asked, keenly.

'I just know. He'd never do anything like that.'

Clare nodded. She hadn't really expected Sharon to be able to produce anything more substantial than her faith in Burley's innocence. If she'd possessed evidence, the police would have known at an early stage.

Clare let her gaze go round the small, untidy room. It was always possible that £20,000 was hidden somewhere within its confines, but she didn't think it probable. Whether or not Burley was guilty, Clare was sure that his fiancée's belief in his innocence was not stimulated.

'How did Steve get on with Miss Sharman?'

'He never did her any harm. In fact, he quite liked her. They all did.'

'Can he think of any reason why she should have identified him as the man who ran past her with the money?'

Sharon shook her head in a bewildered way. 'She was mistaken. She must have been mistaken. It wasn't him.'

'But she's absolutely certain it was. And the jury believed her.'

'It couldn't have been Steve. He was out at lunch. He was nowhere near the office at the time. He called witnesses to say that.'

Clare had gathered from Nick that the defence had, indeed, called two witnesses in an attempt to prove Burley's presence elsewhere, but they turned out to be vague as to times and, in the event, their evidence had helped no one. In fact, in Nick's view it had been worse than useless as it tended to give the jury the impression of a botched alibi.

'Have you yourself ever met Miss Sharman?' The girl shook her head. 'Or Mr Rickard?'

'No.'

'Did Steve talk about them much?'

'No, why should he?'

'Did he enjoy his work at Rickard's?'

'He wasn't going to stay there after we were married.'

'Did he have any particular friend?'

'No. He got on with everyone.'

'So he didn't have any enemies either?'

'Absolutely not.'

'How long have you known him, Sharon?'

'A year on the fifteenth of next month,' she replied, as though it were the one answer she didn't have to ponder.

'This is rather a personal question, but what is your money situation? I mean, getting married can be an expensive business.'

'I've got £300 in my savings account.'

'And Steve?'

'He'd just bought a car. He got it cheap through Rickard's.'

'Was he worried about not having money?'

'Why should he have been worried?' Sharon asked with a sudden note of asperity. 'We both had jobs. We're young. We could have managed. My mum and dad got married when they were both nineteen and dad was earning five pounds a week on the land.' She gave Clare a sharp look. 'Is that what you've really come about, money? Because, if so, we don't need anyone's charity. All we want is justice.'

'I only mentioned money as part of a general enquiry,' Clare said quickly and got up. She decided she had better leave before the girl began to probe her credentials further. Moreover, she felt that she had found out as much as she could on a first visit. She gave Sharon her home telephone number and told her to call if she needed any advice or help.

It seemed to Clare that Sharon Pratt had created a small world just large enough to hold herself and her Steve and that she was basically uninterested in anything which didn't affect it.

As she walked away from the house, Clare reflected that an interview with Eva Sharman was going to be a very different proposition. Though the challenge exhilarated her, the difficulty and perhaps even danger were daunting. For if it did emerge as possible that Miss Sharman had made a deliberately false identification, there would be no knowing how far the evil might have seeped.

CHAPTER THREE

Having spent the morning catching up with paper work at his station on X Division – that was the trouble with days in Court, the work piled up on your desk – Nick set off soon after two o'clock for Scotland Yard. If he could dispose of the matters which took him there in time, he had it in mind to phone Stephen Burley's defence counsel and ask if he might drop by and see him for a few minutes. The Temple, where David Chant had his chambers, was only ten minutes away from the Yard and it would be convenient if he could incorporate the two visits, the more so as his approach to Burley's counsel was unofficial. It was possible that Chant would decline to talk to him, but Nick felt he had, at least, to make the effort.

As events turned out, he completed his business at the Yard more quickly than he had expected and was about to leave the building in search of a public call box when he bumped into Detective Sergeant Tarry by the lifts.

Nick and Tom Tarry were of the same age and had done their initial training together. Since then, their paths had often crossed, though they had never actually served together. They had, however, retained the sort of easy friendship that caused them to greet each other with pleasure when chance brought about a meeting.

'Hello, Nick,' Sergeant Tarry called out cheerfully as he came up behind him. 'Believe it or not, I was going to ring you in the next day or two. How's life over on X?'

'Busy, but it could be a lot worse. And what about you, Tom?'

'You know how it is with us. We dig, burrow and swoop,' Tarry said with a grin, referring to the sort of target operations undertaken by the Serious Crimes Squad of which he was a member. 'On the whole, I reckon we earn our keep.'

Nick glanced at his watch. It was only just four o'clock

and the odds were that David Chant wouldn't yet be back in chambers from Court.

'If you've got a few minutes, Tom, why don't we go up to the canteen?'

'Good idea and I can tell you what I was going to call you about.'

Armed with cups of tea, they went and sat at a table away from other people.

'I tell you what it was, Nick,' Tarry said, stirring his tea vigorously, 'I believe you recently had a case involving someone called Miles Rickard?'

Nick nodded and felt his interest quicken. 'He was a witness for the prosecution in a trial which only finished at the Old Bailey yesterday. He's the managing director of Rickard Motor Distributors Limited whose premises are at Greenford on my manor. They lost £20,000 in a burglary and one of their young clerks has just been sent down for three years. Anyway, what's your interest in him, Tom?'

'I'm not sure at the moment. It could be only peripheral, it could fizzle out altogether. On the other hand, it could grow.' He reached into his pocket and extracted a packet of cigarettes. He proffered it to Nick who shook his head. 'Still don't smoke? Wish I didn't, lousy, dirty . . . comforting habit! What do you know of Rickard's background, Nick?'

'That he's married and has a stepson in his early twenties who's an actor. That his wife is one of those perennial middle-aged blondes with, I would imagine, expensive tastes and that he inherited the business from his father who died suddenly of a coronary about six years ago. I think that's about all. I saw him about half a dozen times in connection with the case and he was always helpful and co-operative. He struck me as being rather an unaggressive man for that particular trade and his whole attitude toward the burglary could be summed up as one of sorrow more than anger.'

'Did he ever give the impression of having problems on his mind?'

'What businessman doesn't these days?' Nick replied.

'That's true. There's a lot to be said for a regular monthly pay cheque, even if it wouldn't keep an Arab in worry beads.' Tom Tarry finished his tea and leaned forward resting his

21

elbows on the table. 'Does the name Wenner mean anything to you, Nick?'

'I think I've heard the name, but I can't connect it with anything,' Nick said after a pause.

'There's a father and son, Frank and Alec Wenner. They own a nightclub called the Crimson Turban. It's off Bond Street. They also own a large block of flats in Maida Vale and various other properties and made a mint of money when the going was good. Recently, they're believed to have moved in on the porn trade.'

'Hence your interest in them?'

Sergeant Tarry nodded. 'Frank Wenner's been a cunning old boy and, though his son's less subtle, he's every bit as ruthless. They're both considerably feared in the shady world in which they operate, but so far they've managed to stay outside of the law's reach. We've had them in and out of our sights for some time, but it's now been decided on high that we ought to dig a little deeper and see if we can't wrong-foot them.'

'I remember now,' Nick said, 'I have heard the name. It was four or five years ago when I had a short spell at West End Central.'

'That figures. But you've not heard it more recently?'

'No, I don't think so. Should I have?'

'Well, you might have,' Tarry said, watching the puzzled expression on Nick's face. 'There's a third member of the family I've not mentioned. Frank Wenner's daughter, Helen, who keeps house for her father and brother. The mother died several years ago. But I gather you've not heard of Helen Wenner either?'

'No, I'm sure I haven't.'

'I thought you might have. She changed her name back to Wenner when her marriage broke up, but she used to be Helen Rickard.'

'You mean she was once married to Miles Rickard?'

Sergeant Tarry nodded. 'My information is that she married him against the wishes of her father, who had always idolised her, and that his lack of enthusiasm for his son-in-law turned to bitter hatred when Rickard failed to treat his wife as a good man should. I don't think he physically ill-treated her, but I

22

gather he philandered and made her very unhappy and that finally she left him and got a divorce. It was about the time her mother died and she went back home to look after her father and brother. Old man Wenner insisted she should drop the name of Rickard and revert to her maiden name which she did.' He gave Nick a quick glance. 'You didn't learn any of this in the course of your burglary enquiry?'

'No reason why I should have. All I know about Miles Rickard's domestic circumstances is what he told me in the course of conversation. I've heard somewhere that he had been married before, and I realised that his present wife had also had a previous marriage because of the stepson he referred to.' Nick paused and then said with a puzzled frown, 'But I'm still not clear, Tom, what your real interest is in Rickard.'

'As I've indicated, nor are we, Nick. But rumour has it that old man Wenner swore revenge against Rickard for the way he'd treated Helen and even that he has attempted to put pressure on his ex-son-in-law in various unspecified ways. And Frank Wenner is not the sort of man to make idle threats or to feud with unless you have an atomic shelter to hide in. Anyway, Nick, we'll keep in touch. Could be we can help each other.'

'Sure, Tom. It's been very interesting what you've told me. Very interesting indeed.'

Together they went down in the lift and parted company outside the main entrance. There was a post office on the other side of the road and Nick went across to make his call to David Chant.

He got through to the clerk's office and asked to speak to Mr Chant. A moment later the connection was made.

'Are you phoning to tell me there's been a gross miscarriage of justice and that the Home Secretary is about to release my client?' Chant asked with heavy humour.

Nick gave a nervous laugh. 'Not quite that, Mr Chant, but I should very much appreciate a quiet word with you about the case. Would it be convenient if I came along now?'

There was a silence before Chant said, 'I suppose so. Yes, all right.'

A quarter of an hour later, Nick was walking up the stone

stairway which led to Chant's second floor chambers in Mulberry Court. He noticed from the list of names painted on the black, solid outer door that David Chant's was one from the bottom. One of the junior clerks led him along a passage to a door at the end and knocked. It was a small room containing three desks on each of which briefs were laid out to suggest a competition as to which of the room's occupants could cover the greatest area with paper.

At this moment, however, David Chant was the only person in the room. He rose as Nick entered and waved him to a chair. Without his barrister's wig, he looked even younger. Really no more than a sixth former, reflected Nick who at thirty-two felt suddenly ancient.

Chant saw Nick glance at the other two desks and said, 'It's all right, the two I share this room with are both out, so we shan't be disturbed.' He gave Nick a quizzical smile. 'I gathered more from your tone than from what you actually said that you wanted to talk to me privately? You realise, of course, that I no longer have any standing in the case. It's over and my instructions are at an end, though I do gather I'll probably be asked to advise on the question of an appeal in due course. Having said that, you'd better tell me what brings you on this unusual visit.'

'I'm rather in the same position, Mr Chant. I mean, the case is over as far as the police are concerned and I ought to make it quite clear that I'm not here as anyone's emissary and that my visit is entirely on my own initiative. I hope that doesn't embarrass you?'

'Not yet,' Chant replied with an attractive smile. 'Go ahead and I'll let you know when I think we're straying into dangerous water.'

For a few seconds Nick seemed to wrestle with his thoughts, then he took a deep breath and said, 'I'm wondering if the jury reached the right result yesterday.'

Chant's head went back as if he had received a knock under the chin.

'I should have thought that was my worry more than yours,' he said with a note of chill. 'What reason do you have for doubting the verdict?'

'It's just a feeling, sir,' Nick said helplessly.

24

'You're not suggesting that the jury was got at?'

'No, no, nothing like that.'

'Well, what is it you *are* suggesting?'

Nick sighed. He did wish that barristers didn't so readily assume their cross-examining manner out of court.

'I'm not *suggesting* anything, sir. It's just that I've had this growing feeling that your client may have been innocent.'

He gave Chant an appealing look, but to no apparent avail.

'Then you must be suggesting that Miss Sharman was mistaken in her evidence; even that she committed perjury?'

'What was your impression of her, sir?' Nick asked, slipping out of the witness-box into which counsel had thrust him.

'Very plausible. Very persuasive. But she could still have been lying.'

'I have no evidence that she was.'

'The whole case rested on her testimony and she won the day for you.'

Nick winced. It seemed as if Burley's counsel was determined not to make his task easier.

'Look, sir, I'm probably not putting this very well, but the reason I've come to see you is because I'm unhappy about what's happened.'

'So what are you going to do about it?'

'There's nothing I can do officially. Your client's been convicted and it's up to him to appeal if he wants to. That's the official attitude. So far as the police are concerned, the case is closed; at any rate for the time being. What I'd really like to know is whether you share my feeling, sir?'

'Now, we're approaching deeper water,' Chant said, with a slight grimace. 'I don't have to tell you, Sergeant Attwell, that a barrister's role is to advance everything that can be said on behalf of his client. He doesn't put forward a personal view. Moreover, I was always taught never to identify myself with my client's cause. Detachment is an advocate's watchword.'

'I know all that, sir, but I've stuck my neck out coming to see you today and I hoped you might feel able to confirm or dispel the anxieties I've formed.'

'But you still haven't told me why you've formed them?'

Nick groaned inwardly. 'In the first place, Burley has never wavered in his denial of the offence. He has always maintained that it was a case of mistaken identity and I was impressed by his demeanour during the trial and in the way he gave his evidence. And then his faint at the end seemed genuine and . . . oh, I don't know, sir, it's a host of tiny impressions all adding up to an uneasy feeling.'

'I wish you'd been on the jury,' Chant said, with a small smile, and lapsed into a thoughtful silence. When he spoke again, his tone was much friendlier. 'It's really a matter of conscience that's brought you here?'

'Correct, sir.'

'But unless you can get your superiors interested, what can you do on your own?'

'Just dig around in my spare time and hope to find something that'll remove my doubts one way or the other.'

'And you're prepared to do that?'

'Yes.'

'If I may say so, aren't you a rather unusual police officer?'

'I don't think I am. Admittedly we're not all identically programmed, but then neither are the members of the legal profession.'

'Thank God!' Chant said in a tone which made Nick think he might have misjudged him. Then leaning back in his chair and staring thoughtfully at the book-lined wall behind Nick, he went on slowly, 'Well, let me see if I can match your frankness with my own.' His gaze left the book shelves and came to rest on Nick. 'I also thought my client was an impressive witness and I can tell you that his defence was mistaken identity from beginning to end. He never once shifted ground the three or four times I saw him in conference. I think probably that if it had remained a straight contest between him and Miss Sharman, he might have been acquitted on the burden of proof issue. It's possible, anyway. But, of course, our two witnesses didn't help. When it came to it, they admitted in cross-examination that their timings might be a bit out and once that happened we were sunk. Well, not sunk perhaps, but at a heavy disadvantage.' He smiled ruefully. 'I'm not being wise after the event – after all, I've hardly begun in the profession – but I did warn Burley and my instructing solicitor that a failed alibi is worse than no alibi. But it was Burley himself, encouraged by his girl, who was insistent that they be called.' Chant paused. 'And if he knew he was innocent, who can blame him? He knew he wasn't in the building when the burglary took place and here were two witnesses who could confirm that he was elsewhere. The only thing was they couldn't – at least, not conclusively. And that was damning in the eyes of a jury.' He expelled a lungful of air. 'Frankly, I don't know what to think. Certainly if Burley had got off, I'd never have said he was a lucky fellow as one frequently does in respect of one's acquitted clients. Equally, as the evidence came out, I couldn't say he was unlucky. He had a fair trial and though, of course, he wants to appeal, heaven knows what grounds we can find. The judge summed up impeccably, even though I don't like the old bastard. I suppose our only hope is to hammer the mistaken identity point. It's a fashionable one to take these days.' He shook his head gloomily. 'The difficulty is I don't see how we can suggest Miss Sharman was mistaken. Innocently mistaken, that is. She saw that tell-tale scar beneath his eye through the slit in his mask. Also she recognised his jacket. How could she have been mistaken about those details?' He paused. 'Of course, it's a different matter if she *deliberately* made a false identification.'

'Did Burley ever suggest that she had?'

Chant shook his head. 'Not once. He just gave the impression of being bewildered by what had happened to him.'

'That's how he always struck me. Doesn't that show something?'

'Either that he's remarkably simple or an excellent actor.'

'Or that he was innocent.'

'Yes or that,' Chant agreed.

As Nick walked to the Temple Underground Station, he cast his mind over the afternoon's events. His chance meeting with Tom Tarry had been much more profitable than his visit to Burley's counsel. It had been like a plate of juicy scraps slapped down in front of a hungry dog.

He couldn't wait to get home and tell Clare and to find out how her meeting with Sharon Pratt had gone.

Curiously, his thoughts about Clare engineering an interview with Eva Sharman ran along much the same lines as Clare's own. Though, in his case, they were better founded in the light of his knowledge of the Wenner connection with Rickard.

If Eva Sharman *had* committed deliberate perjury and sent an innocent man to prison, he was quite certain that she had not done so on her own initiative.

CHAPTER FOUR

Miles Rickard lighted a fresh cigarette from the butt of the previous one and inhaled deeply. The morning wasn't half-way gone and his ash tray was already overflowing. From being a heavy smoker, he had become a chain smoker. The days he had spent in Court had been hell with their enforced abstinence.

His office was one of five immediately above the showroom. There was a staircase at each end of the passage that ran outside. One led down into the back of the showroom, the other to a door which opened on to a street which flanked the side of his premises.

Eva Sharman had the room next to his and he could hear her typewriter going at full blast. On the other side of him lay the sales manager's office. The remaining rooms were occupied by two typists and the clerks.

Rickard rose from his desk and walked across to the window which overlooked the forecourt, where Fred, the odd-job man, was giving a large B.M.W. one of his extra special polishes. Rickard knew that the purchaser was coming in to collect it in about an hour's time and would be paying for it in cash. Much of his business was transacted in cash these days and it was commonplace for customers to count out bundles of ten- and twenty-pound notes which they extracted from briefcases, airline bags and even plastic carriers whose previous contents had probably been fish fingers and frozen peas.

The business which his father had founded had in recent years been concentrated on the sale of expensive second-hand cars whose mileage was so small as to make them almost new.

He was still gazing moodily down on the gleaming roof of the B.M.W. when his telephone buzzed.

'I have Mrs Rickard on the line,' Miss Sharman announced in an impersonal tone, 'shall I put her through?'

'Yes.'

'Miles, I thought I'd let you know that Terry and I have decided to go into town. There's some new movie Terry wants to see and I thought we'd give ourselves a slap-up lunch first. I might also do a bit of shopping.'

'All right, darling, have a nice day,' Rickard said without great enthusiasm. With a forced laugh he added, 'And don't spend too much money!'

It wasn't that he begrudged Pamela anything, but when she and his stepson went out on the town together, restraint was seldom their watchword.

'See you this evening, Miles. Don't forget the Whickers are coming in for drinks at half past six. I think I'll buy a bit of smoked salmon and make a few canapés. If I get enough, we can finish it up at dinner. You know what Terry's like with smoked salmon. It doesn't go very far when he's around.'

Not for the first time, Rickard reflected that an indigent young actor had no right to have such expensive tastes as his stepson exhibited.

With a final exchange of endearments, the call concluded. He was still reflecting on it when there was a soft knock on his door.

'Come in,' he said in an abstracted tone. Several moments passed before he realised that his visitor had not materialised in front of his desk. Swinging round sharply, he found himself staring at Alec Wenner who was standing, looking down at him with a small amused smile.

'Hello, Miles. Happened to be in the area and thought I'd drop in and see how business was,' Wenner said, sweeping the office with a dispassionate gaze.

'Business is all right.'

'Glad to hear it. Lucky you. Not everyone's doing well these days. Good to hear you are, particularly as Frank and I still hold a few shares in the company.'

'I hadn't forgotten.'

'I'm sure you hadn't, Miles. Maybe we could increase our interest. Frank was saying so again the other day.'

30

Rickard could not fail to note the faintly menacing emphasis which was given to 'again'.

'I doubt whether there's any scope for that,' he said, uncomfortably.

'I don't think that Frank would like to hear himself turned down as flatly as that, Miles. For that matter, I don't either.' His gaze roamed once more round Rickard's office. 'We heard about your burglary, of course,' he remarked, his tongue scavenging round his front teeth. 'How much was it the chap got away with?'

'Twenty thousand pounds,' Rickard said, well aware that Wenner knew the answer to his question.

'That's quite a sum,' Wenner replied in a bored tone. 'Could have been a nasty knock to your profits if you hadn't been insured.' He fixed Rickard with a quizzical look. 'I take it you were insured?'

'It's a question of interpretation of the policy,' Rickard said unconvincingly. 'I'm in touch with the insurance company about it.'

Wenner frowned. 'I don't like the sound of that, Miles. What are you going to tell your shareholders? Some of them won't like it either. You'd better make sure that the insurance company does pay up.'

Rickard made no reply. All he could do was to roll with the punches. He knew that the sole object of Wenner's visit was to remind him that they lurked, an ever potent force, in the background of his life. Not that he was likely to forget anyway.

'Of course,' Wenner went on, 'there are worse things than burglaries. At least no one got hurt in your burglary.' He shook his head slowly. 'But that's worrying about the insurance, isn't it? I wonder if the burglar could have known he was giving you a double knock?' He strolled over to the window and gazed down on the forecourt. 'I'm thinking of getting another car myself. A Merc., I think. You might look around for me, Miles.' He grinned. 'But remember these are hard times, so none of your fancy prices. Anyway, as your ex-brother-in-law, I expect a decent discount.'

The door opened and Eva Sharman came in holding some papers. She was about to back out, when Wenner said in his

31

most cordial tone, 'Don't go, Miss Sharman. I'm afraid I butted in unannounced, but I'm just off. How are you, my dear?'

'Very well, thank you, Mr Wenner.'

'You're luckier than you realise, Miles. How much easier all our lives would be if each of us had the support of a Miss Sharman! I know mine would be. Hope I've not made you blush, my dear!' He moved toward the door. 'Well, bear our little chat in mind, Miles, and either I or Frank will be in touch with you again before long. So long, Miss Sharman.'

'I hope I didn't interrupt,' Eva Sharman said after he had left. 'I had no idea he was with you.'

'He just walked in,' Rickard said wearily. 'I suppose the side door must have been unlocked.' He glanced at the papers in her hand. 'What have you got there, Eva?'

'They're the letters you dictated yesterday evening. I still have two more to type, but I'm gradually getting straight again. Those three days in Court put me right behind.' She gave a small shiver. 'That's not an experience I ever wish to repeat.'

'You were a very good witness. Everyone said so. But for you he'd almost certainly have got away with it.'

'It's still not an experience that I wish to repeat,' she said firmly and left the room.

CHAPTER FIVE

Since her mother's death eight years ago, Eva Sharman had lived alone in a small flat with a large tabby cat called Mott for company. Its unusual name had happened to be that of the lady who had given it to her when it was only a kitten. Miss Sharman had felt that it deserved a rather special name and had called it Mott while she tried to think up a suitable appellation. However, as time went by and she would think of a name only to discard it, the cat itself settled the issue by clearly accepting its temporary name.

It was a ground-floor flat in a neat terraced row in Ealing and not much more than a ten minute bus ride from her place of work.

She was invariably home by six o'clock each evening and seldom went out again unless it was to call on an invalid friend or go to the pictures.

She had always been very fond of the cinema, particularly thrillers and most particularly of all of Alfred Hitchcock's films. She'd even go up to the West End on a Saturday afternoon to see his latest offering.

But these irregular outings apart, she stayed at home and watched television or would pick a magazine from the pile beside her chair. Her knowledge of what was going on in the world came principally from reading magazines. She never looked at a book, but would read a magazine from cover to cover and then put it back on the pile for further perusal at a later date.

Clare had watched Miss Sharman get off the bus and had kept her under discreet observation as she walked the remaining hundred yards to her home. She decided to give her twenty minutes before ringing the front-door bell. Twenty minutes to take off her hat and coat, to give herself a cup of tea and to attend to whatever were her first necessities on arrival home.

As a result of his conversation with Tom Tarry, Nick had swung right against his original idea that Clare should talk to Eva Sharman.

'The Wenner connection gives the case a new dimension,' he had said. 'There could be danger and I'm not going to have you exposing yourself to any sort of risk.' And he had expanded on this theme.

'You make Eva Sharman sound like a blend of Lucrezia Borgia and Annie Oakley,' Clare had replied. 'And I don't believe she's either. Anyway, that's what I'm going to find out.' She had paused before clinching their argument by saying, 'Having reorganised my life and got rid of Simon for a few days, you can't suddenly turn me off like a tap. Not when it was you who turned me on in the first place.'

Once Clare had made her determination clear, they had discussed how she should approach the meeting.

In the end they had agreed that she should pretend to be a friend of Sharon Pratt and should confront Eva Sharman on the basis that somehow there must have been a dreadful mistake. It was felt that such a direct approach must draw a reaction from her, hopefully one which would provide a clue as to her true role.

Having spent a good deal of her police service acting as comforter to the wives and girl-friends of those caught up in the criminal law, Clare liked to believe that she played the part well. She had a naturally sympathetic manner so that it had never become a question of pure acting. Some people are born confidantes and she was one such.

She glanced at her watch and decided the moment had come. Giving a hitch to her shoulder bag, she marched up to Miss Sharman's front door and knocked. As she did so, Mott appeared from nowhere and began rubbing himself against her legs. She stooped to stroke him just as Miss Sharman opened the door.

'There you are!' she exclaimed, as Mott streaked inside the house. Then looking up at Clare, she said, 'Was he on the step when you arrived?'

'I don't know where he came from, he just appeared when I knocked. He seems a very friendly cat,' Clare said, smiling.

'Oh, he is. He's normally always waiting for me when I get

34

home in the evening, but today I couldn't find him anywhere. Oh, well,' she added with a shrug, 'I expect he had his own affairs to attend to. But I'm so sorry prattling on like this . . . you've called to see me about something?'

'Yes,' Clare said with an air of diffidence which was only partly simulated. 'My name's Clare Reynolds, I'm a friend of Stephen Burley's fiancée. I doubt whether I have any right to bother you, but we are all so worried about what has happened that I felt I must at least try and see you. If you shut the door in my face, I'll quite understand, though I shall be most grateful if I can have a few words with you.'

Clare found herself staring back at a suddenly expressionless face. For the first time she was able to take in its features. The iron grey hair pulled back into a small bun, the sallow cheeks and thin mouth, the nose which looked a size too large for the rest of the face and the pair of horn-rimmed spectacles which rested on it. And behind the spectacles, the cool, appraising eyes, which were looking Clare up and down.

It seemed to Clare that she waited an age before Miss Sharman made any reply.

'You'd better come in, though I doubt whether I can help you very much.'

Her tone matched the absence of enthusiasm in her words. Nevertheless, Clare let out a small sigh of relief. At least the door had not been slammed in her face. With murmured thanks she stepped past Miss Sharman into the hall and then stood aside waiting to be shown which room to enter. Not that there appeared to be a great choice, there being only two doors leading off the hall.

The room into which Miss Sharman took her could not have been more different from Sharon Pratt's. It was as neat and tidy as the other was disordered. In one corner was a divan bed overlaid with a fitted brown cover, on which rested half a dozen small square velvet cushions of different bright colours.

'What an attractive arrangement!' Clare said admiringly.

'You have to do something when you live and sleep in the one room,' Miss Sharman replied with a note of pleasure. 'I always eat in my little kitchen, so at least I don't have food smells in here.'

35

Deciding that their relationship was too fragile to sustain unlimited small talk, Clare plunged in.

'As I said, I've come about Stephen Burley. We just can't believe he really did it and feel there must have been some ghastly mistake. Do you think it's possible it was someone else?' Her words came out in a rush and with a note of anguish. 'It's so easy to be mistaken and then it gets fixed in one's mind and in no time at all a false impression becomes a certainty of recollection. It's awful cheek on my part to suggest this, but we feel desperate about Steve and decided we had to do something to try and help him. It was because you were so fair in Court and, if I may say so, looked such a nice person that we decided to talk to you first and see whether you mayn't have felt any doubts about what happened?'

It was several seconds before Eva Sharman replied, her attention apparently distracted by the arrival of Mott who stalked into the room with tail in the air and made an immediate leap into Clare's lap. She hoped his owner might, metaphorically, follow suit.

'If I'd had any doubts,' Miss Sharman said slowly, 'I'd have declared them. I liked Stephen from what little I knew of him. He was an agreeable young man.'

'Were you surprised at what he did?'

'Very surprised.'

'And yet you're certain it was he?'

'There's no doubt at all.'

'But the burglar was wearing a mask, wasn't he?'

'He was also wearing Stephen's jacket. It was the jacket he always wore to work, a small black and white check. But it was the scar that really gave him away. The eye-holes had been cut quite large and there was his scar. I could see it clearly. There was absolutely no mistaking it.'

'It must have been a terrifying moment for both of you.'

'I can only speak for myself. I just happened to come out of my office and there he was slipping away from Mr Rickard's. He half-tripped and we came face to face.'

'I gather he didn't speak?'

'Not a word. He just stared at me for a second as he recovered himself and then ran off down the stairs that lead to the side entrance.'

'Did he appear frightened himself? From the look in his eyes, I mean?'

'That would be my impression. But if you were at the trial, why are you asking me all these questions? You must have heard me give my evidence.'

'I only heard the final stages of the trial. I didn't hear you in the witness box. Looking back now, Miss Sharman, on the whole sequence of events, do you feel there's any possibility of a mistake having been made?'

'I'm sorry for you and all Stephen's friends, but there was no mistake.' And she compressed her lips in firm, implacable lines as though to prevent the escape of further words.

It was apparent to Clare that the soft approach was not going to get her any further. The question was whether to accept the position and withdraw politely or whether to adopt a blunter line. In the event, Clare decided that to do so would lose her nothing. After all, she was not planning to make a friend for life in Eva Sharman.

'I believe you've worked for Rickard's for over thirty years?' she remarked.

'I began with the present Mr Rickard's father just after the war,' the other woman replied with a faint note of pride. 'Of course, Mr Miles Rickard was only a schoolboy at that time.'

'You obviously know the family pretty well, Miss Sharman. Has it been your impression that Mr Rickard has recently had problems on his mind?'

'Is that what Stephen has been telling his friends? I don't think you should listen to that sort of gossip, Miss Reynolds. Stephen couldn't have known anything about Mr Rickard's private life.'

But Eva Sharman clearly did! Clare felt a sudden tingle of excitement. She hadn't mentioned Miles Rickard's *private* life, but this was the assumption which his secretary had immediately made.

'I gathered,' Clare went on more determinedly, 'it was common knowledge that Mr Rickard's first wife was still making difficulties for him. Or rather that her father was. Wenner? Isn't that the name?'

'You can't possibly expect me to discuss my employer's private life with you, Miss Reynolds.' Her tone was sharp, though Clare felt it was a sharpness to hide embarrassment.

'If it had anything to do with sending an innocent person to prison, it would be your duty to do so, wouldn't it?'

Now the cards were really down. Miss Sharman gave a small gasp and stood up.

'I can see no point in continuing this conversation. What is more, I am sure Stephen's friends don't help him by being inquisitive about matters that don't concern him.'

Clare had to remove a reluctant Mott from her lap before she could get out of her chair. Moving to the door, she said, 'I'm sorry if I've upset you, Miss Sharman, but such is my anxiety over what's happened to Steve that I had to run that risk.' She held out her hand. 'Nevertheless, I'm grateful to you for talking to me.' She paused. 'Perhaps it has given us both food for thought.'

Miss Sharman gave her hand a perfunctory shake and stalked to the front door.

Clare suppressed a smile. She only needed a tail high in the air to match the affront being exhibited by her cat.

After Eva Sharman had locked the door she returned to the room and peered cautiously out of the window. She half-expected to see Clare still lingering outside. It was in a thoughtful mood that she made her way to the kitchen. She had, indeed, been given food for thought.

Of one thing she was convinced. The so-called Miss Reynolds had never belonged to Stephen Burley's set of friends.

CHAPTER SIX

When Nick received a message from Wormwood Scrubs Prison that Stephen Burley wished to see him, he went immediately to Detective Chief Superintendent Rudgwick to tell him.

To Rudgwick, who knew nothing of Nick's worries about the case, it had been a quickly solved crime with the jury returning a sensible verdict. He wished that all the cases on his division gave as little trouble.

Nick, for his part, welcomed the opportunity of being able to go and see Burley with official approval.

'Any idea what it's about?' Rudgwick enquired, glancing with distaste at the pile of paper in his in-tray.

'No, sir, but it can only be that he's remembered something that he thinks will assist him.'

'Why doesn't he tell his solicitor then? They can raise it on appeal. What are we expected to do with the information at this stage?'

'Depends on what it is, sir.'

'If it's what you believe, I'd have thought it better he passed it on to his own legal advisers.'

'I may be wrong, sir. It could be something quite different.'

'Such as?'

'I don't know, sir.'

'Nor do I.' Rudgwick frowned. 'You don't think it's a complaint against police?'

Nick was sure that his Detective Chief Superintendent had not deliberately touched this tender spot; indeed, it was apparent that his blush went unnoticed as Rudgwick continued to stare gloomily at the top of his desk.

'I hardly think he'd have asked to see me personally, sir, if it were to complain about my handling of the case.'

'Unlikely, I agree,' Rudgwick remarked. 'Anyway, there's

no shortage of advice in prison these days on how to lodge complaints against the police. It won't be long before they establish hot lines between A.10 and all the penal establishments in the M.P.D.' He looked up. 'Well, all right, Nick, if he's asked to see you, you'd better find out what he wants. But be careful! More police officers have been led up more blind alleys as a result of visiting convicted men in prison than in any other way. Always remember that your prisoner is above all bored. He'll do anything to relieve the monotony of his day and having a policeman dancing attendance is a particularly appealing form of entertainment.'

'I'll have that in mind, sir,' Nick said, relieved that he had, at least, received his guvnor's consent to make the visit. He was about to go when Rudgwick spoke again.

'By the way, I've had a call from Commander Bridges of C.I. saying that the Serious Crimes Squad are showing an interest in Frank Wenner and he'd be glad of any local co-operation required. Wenner moved house earlier this year and now lives in a far-flung corner of this manor. His daughter was once married to Miles Rickard.'

'So I learnt yesterday, sir. I happened to bump into Detective Sergeant Tarry when I was up at the Yard and he told me of their interest. I'm afraid Wenner's name didn't really ring a bell with me.'

'You've not been on the division long enough. Anyway, he hasn't given us any trouble. He's one of the big-time boys, he'd consider it beneath his dignity to be investigated by any local copper. As a matter of fact, I'd completely forgotten that Rickard's first wife was Wenner's daughter. Or I should put it the other way about, that Wenner's daughter had been married to Rickard, as I've never had any occasion to meet Rickard. He doesn't sell the sort of cars I can afford.' He squinted at Nick round the spiral of smoke from his cigarette. 'You didn't have any trouble from Rickard in the course of your enquiries, did you?'

Nick shook his head. 'None, sir, he was most co-operative.'

'And Wenner's name never cropped up?'

'No, sir, it didn't even ring a bell with me when Sergeant Tarry mentioned it yesterday.'

'I remember, you said that just now.' He picked up a file

from his desk, stared at it and then let it drop back on top of others. 'Shall I tell you something? I retire in four months' time and I'm not going to miss any of this one little bit.' As he spoke, his hand swept round his office. 'I'll have done my thirty and I'll be off. Off back to Norfolk where I started life and where the toughest rats don't always win the race.'

'I hope good luck accompanies you, sir.'

'Give me decent health and you can keep the luck.' He stubbed out his cigarette and said briskly, 'When are you planning to visit Burley?'

'I thought I'd go this afternoon, sir.'

Wormwood Scrubs in west London was the nearest prison to Nick's divisional station. Using back streets it took him less than twenty minutes to get there.

Though he had on many occasions entered all of London's prisons, he had never got used to the echoing sounds of their great halls of confinement. The Scrubs might have an air of spaciousness which was denied the others, but this was no more than an illusion created by the fact that it was less hemmed in than other prisons. Within its walls, however, the atmosphere was still that generated by men forcibly locked up by society, the dangerous, the weak and the unfortunate being herded together in one uneasy brotherhood.

Nick was shocked by Burley's appearance when he was escorted into the interview room. He had been in the Scrubs only three days, but he had a pasty appearance with dark rings round his eyes which had a feverish look. The scar beneath his right eye now seemed to give his face an almost sinister expression. And the rough, ill-fitting prison clothes only served to emphasise the degradation he had suffered.

To Nick, who was inclined to believe him innocent, the shock of his appearance was even greater than it might have been.

'I got your message, Steve,' he said, as Burley sat down facing him. 'What is it you want to see me about?'

'I'm glad you came,' Burley said, attempting a smile. 'I've thought of one or two things you'll have to investigate.' He put a hand up to his face and began to pick nervously at a pimple on the side of his chin. 'It's the rotten food,' he re-

41

marked savagely, 'I haven't had a spot on my face since I was a kid and now I'm breaking out all over.'

'What are the things you've thought of?' Nick asked quietly.

'Things about that Sharman bitch. She's the one who ought to be in prison with all her scheming lies. You know she used to be old Rickard's mistress?'

'Who are you referring to as *old* Rickard?'

'The present one's father.' He leaned forward and fixed Nick with a look of fierce intensity. 'If you dig around a bit, Mr Attwell, you'll find that Eva Sharman is Miles Rickard's mother.'

'What evidence do you have of that?'

'It was common knowledge.'

'Who told you?'

'I can't remember now, but everyone knew.'

'And supposing I do discover that she is Rickard's mother?' Nick said cautiously.

'It'll prove I was framed.'

'I'm sorry, Steve, but I don't follow that.'

'Rickard was up to some funny business and she supported him.'

'But why should she have pointed her finger at *you*?'

'A bloody poison finger it was! Anyway, that's what I want you to find out.'

'Give me the name of anyone at Rickard's who also knows about Miss Sharman having been old Rickard's mistress and possibly this one's mother.'

'I tell you, it was common knowledge. Ask anyone there!'

'Why haven't you mentioned this before, Steve?'

'I didn't want to sling mud unless I was forced to,' he said, lowering his eyes.

'Did you tell your solicitor?'

Burley shook his head. 'He didn't want to know anything. Look at the way he cocked up my alibi witnesses. They were just nervous, that was all. Why didn't he rehearse them properly?' His tone was bitter.

'I thought your counsel put up a good fight,' Nick remarked.

'Yes, he was all right.'

'Has your solicitor been to see you about an appeal?'

'He gave me a form to fill in, but he was been and gone before you could ask him anything. It was that foxy little clerk of his. This place is full of the likes of him. They either run off with people's savings or touch up small girls. You must know the type, Mr Attwell?'

Nick grinned. 'I reckon I've met my share.'

Burley began picking at his pimple again. 'I must get rid of this thing before Sharon visits. She's coming on Saturday.' He licked the end of his finger and dabbed at it. 'I've asked my parents not to visit me. Not yet, anyway. Perhaps when I'm moved somewhere else. I gather I'll probably go to one of those open prisons.' He glared suddenly. 'Except you've got to get me out before then.'

'Anything else you've thought of?' Nick asked, glancing at his watch.

'I've told you enough, haven't I?' Burley remarked defiantly.

'You said at the beginning that you'd thought of one or two things you wanted to tell me about. You've only mentioned one.'

Burley appeared thoughtful for a moment. 'No, that's all. But you will do your best for me, won't you, Mr Attwell? I've got to get out of here somehow. What sort of justice is it that can keep an innocent man in prison?'

A note of self-pity had replaced his earlier, somewhat truculent tone.

'I'll let you know anything I find out,' Nick said. 'Meanwhile, you be a good boy. Do as you're told! Bend with the wind if you have to! You'll find it makes your existence here less intolerable.'

'Existence! It's hardly that.'

Nick watched him disappear out of the door followed by his escorting officer who had spent the time sitting in a corner of the room, trimming his fingernails.

When Nick arrived home that evening and Clare asked him about his visit to the prison, he said, 'It's left me exactly where I was. There were even one or two moments when I began to wonder if he wasn't making a fool of me. He seemed a different person.'

'So might you become if you found yourself in prison for

something you'd not done. Surely the point is that he didn't say anything to shake your belief in his possible innocence.'

'Nor to confirm it either.'

'It was too much to expect that.'

'Why did you say that?'

'Look at it from his point of view. He's proclaimed his innocence from the outset and he sticks by it. What else can he say to persuade you?'

'Nothing, I suppose.'

'You're not in the mood to give up, are you?' Clare asked with a note of surprise.

'No, I'm not. It's just . . .'

'It's just that a plaintive Stephen Burley in prison clothes with a spot on his face is different from the shining innocent who has captured your imagination.' Clare put out a hand and pushed back a lock of Nick's hair that had fallen forward. 'Anyway, it shouldn't be too difficult to find out whether there's any truth in what he told you about Eva Sharman. *I* can go to St Catherine's House and find out who is recorded as Miles Rickard's mother. You have the date of his birth, don't you?'

'Yes, it's in his statement. While you do that, I'll be questioning Rickard's employees about the other suggestion. I'll have to do it discreetly so that neither Rickard nor Eva Sharman find out.' He shook his head slowly. 'It's difficult to envisage her having ever been anyone's mistress.' He bent forward and kissed Clare. 'This place is like a morgue without Simon. Do you think he's missing us?'

Clare laughed. 'I doubt it. But that doesn't mean he won't be pleased to see us when he gets home.' She returned her husband's kiss. 'Why don't we make the best of his absence and go to Lorenzo's for a plate of Spaghetti Milanese. Before you say no, let me add that, through being out all day, I've let the larder run low. If you're determined to stay in, you'll have to pick a tin and open it.'

'Let's go to Lorenzo's,' he said, giving Clare an affectionate pat on the behind.

CHAPTER SEVEN

Ever since he had been a young lad in the East End, Frank Wenner had made a fetish of physical fitness.

It is often said nowadays of the boys who come before the juvenile courts that, if they took part in some sport, they'd be less likely to drift into crime. Wenner entirely supported this theory and saw nothing inconsistent in the fact that much of his time was spent in outwitting the law.

If anyone had dared to tax him with insincerity, he would have made the point – and made it forcibly – that there was all the difference between casual nuisance crime and the big stuff which was embarked upon as a profitable exercise.

He lived with his son Alec and daughter Helen in a large house on the north-west outskirts of London. It had an acre of garden and a heated swimming pool which had been the reason for his buying it for just over £100,000 eight months before. He had converted a room over the double garage into a gym and every morning while his son and daughter were still in bed, he would put himself through a series of strenuous exercises followed by ten lengths of the pool and a cold shower.

At sixty-three, it was his proud boast that anyone could punch him in the solar plexus and hurt their hand more than his muscle-hard abdomen.

'You need to be fit in my line of business,' he was fond of saying in a tone which defied anyone not to be impressed, regardless of whether they knew to what line of business he was referring.

On this particular morning, he was sitting in the dining alcove with a glass of orange juice before him, waiting impatiently for his son to appear. A few moments later his daughter joined him. She moved his orange juice to one side to make room for the thin slice of toast and two boiled eggs she was carrying. Her father drank the juice without taking the glass from his lips and then set about the eggs. Meanwhile, Helen returned to the table with the pint cup from which he always drank his morning tea.

'What's up with Alec? He gets later every day,' he remarked, sourly.

'He'll be down in a minute. It's only half past eight.'

'Only!'

'Lay off, Dad! Alec works hard.'

'Not as hard as I did at his age.'

'No one works *that* hard,' she said, giving her father an indulgent smile.

'I did it for the old lady and you two kids.'

'Was it worth it?' she asked in a faintly teasing tone.

'Not when you went off and married that little twister, it weren't.'

'That was my mistake, Dad.'

'Wouldn't listen to me, would you, girl?'

'I was in love with him.'

'Treated you like some skivvy. You, Frank Wenner's daughter. Well, he's had a few things to smile about on the other side of his face since then. And he'll have a few more.'

'I've put him out of my life. I don't know why you can't.'

'Because no one humiliates Frank Wenner's daughter and gets away with it. If anyone dares smack my cheek, I don't offer him the other, I clout him one. And go on clouting him for reminders.'

Helen nibbled at a slice of Ryvita and honey, which, with a cup of black coffee, comprised her breakfast. As she now gazed with placid affection at her father, she found it difficult to recall just how unhappy Miles had made her. Once the break had been made and she had returned home, she had been surprised how quickly she had adjusted. So far as she was concerned, her interlude of marriage to Rickard was a gap which was now completely closed. The fact, however, that it wasn't so with her father didn't really trouble her.

' 'Morning, Frank, 'morning, Helen,' Alec Wenner said, bursting into the kitchen.

As a result of their close business association, he had long come to call his father by his first name, though Helen never did so.

'You're late,' Frank Wenner said flatly.

'I didn't get home till three.'

'What were you doing?'

'I met a bird in our club and went back to her place. She was a lively little thing. Even managed to teach me a new trick or two.'

His father frowned. 'Enough of that. You know the old lady wouldn't like that sort of talk.'

Alec threw Helen a rueful look. Along with Frank Wenner's fetish about physical fitness went an obsession about swearing and smutty talk. And although his wife had been dead for over three years, her memory was always invoked to check anything of the sort at home.

Although, too, he moved in circles where expletives ceased to have meaning and dirty stories abounded, Frank Wenner had never participated. He generally ignored all bad language and quickly showed his distaste for blue jokes. There had been more than one occasion when the persistent teller of one had found himself knocked to the floor.

Alec Wenner sat down at the place vacated by his sister, who, in due course, brought him a plate of cereal and some scrambled eggs on toast and a mug of milky coffee.

His father watched him tucking in to his food.

'Why don't you join me in the gym?' he asked suddenly.

'Don't need to. I'm as fit as you are.'

'You're only thirty-four and you're beginning to run to seed.'

'Balls! Sorry, Frank, it slipped out. But I am *not* running to seed. If you weren't my father, I'd stand you up and prove it.'

Frank Wenner didn't speak again until his daughter had gone out of the room. Then he said, 'I've been thinking about your visit to Rickard. It's time we began to put the pressure on him again. So far we've only teased him, now we'll really put the frighteners on.'

'We could certainly do with his co-operation in the near future,' Alec said with a wolf's grin. 'He's got a lot of space

47

at the rear of those premises we could use for storage. I reckon it would be pretty safe, too.'

'Provided he didn't talk out of turn.'

'That's where the frighteners'd come in.'

Frank Wenner grunted. 'It's a good laugh the insurance won't pay up on the burglary.'

'Yeah, I thought that'd amuse you. It was a very nicely set up little job, that burglary. His office safe on the blink and so he puts the money in a drawer of his desk for a couple of hours – and in walks masked burglar and helps himself.'

Frank Wenner began to shake with silent laughter. 'We ought to be madder than we are, seeing we're shareholders.'

'Just what I told him. I said I hoped it wasn't going to affect our dividends,' Alec Wenner said with a broad grin.

'Did you see that monkey, Carmelo, at The Crimson Turban last night?' Frank asked with an abrupt change of mood.

Alec Wenner shook his head. 'He didn't turn up. That's chiefly why I went, to see him.'

'He owes us a couple of thousand. You'd better find him and get it and then tell him to stay away from the place or . . .'

'I'll find him all right. Getting the money may be a bit harder.'

'It shouldn't be beyond your powers. Or do you want me to persuade him to pay his debts?'

'Leave it with me, Frank.'

'I'd like to. Meanwhile, I think I'll pay a little visit to my *ex*-son-in-law.' He spat out the word 'ex' as though it had a bad taste.

CHAPTER EIGHT

Clare's enquiries at St Catherine's House took less time than she
had expected. Moreover, they failed to support the dramatic
suggestion that Eva Sharman might be Miles Rickard's
mother. The records showed that he had been born on Feb-
ruary 27th, 1934, his mother being Dora Olive Rickard and
his father, Arthur Edward Rickard.

The birth had been registered by the father, so there was
still a possibility that he had supplied false details in order
to conceal the true name of the child's mother, but Clare
reckoned this to have been unlikely.

However, it was a detail she could check further if she
could find out where Mrs Rickard senior lived.

Emerging from St Catherine's House, she found the nearest
call box and phoned Nick. He had just returned to the Station
from the scene of a break-in and was eager to have her news.

'I've no idea where she lives,' he said in answer to Clare's
question. 'In fact, I don't even know whether she's still alive.
Miles Rickard never mentioned her, merely that his father
died a few years ago.'

'That in itself might be significant. I mean, that he never
mentioned her.'

'There was no occasion for him to do so. Whereas his
father's death came out in connection with his ownership of
the business. But I can probably find out and I'll let you know
this evening.'

It was with a feeling of frustration that Clare left the call
box and looked for a snack bar to have a cup of coffee while
she decided what to do. She felt like someone all dressed up
with nowhere to go.

Well, she didn't have to wait for Nick to find out the information. She could try and discover it for herself. She knew

Miles Rickard's home address and that would be a good starting-point.

Forty minutes later she was walking along a well-to-do residential road in the neighbourhood of Ealing Common. Many of the houses seemed to be named after Mediterranean pleasure spots, though the Rickards', a 1930s pseudo-Tudor creation, took its name from north of the border. 'Grampians' was painted in large black letters on a moulded board affixed to one of the brick gate posts.

Clare walked up to the front door and rang the bell. She could see a car standing at the entrance to the garage and assumed that someone must be at home.

The door was opened by a young man in his early twenties who gazed at her with one eyebrow cocked and a look which seemed to say, 'I'm amusing, what about you?'

'I'm so sorry to trouble you and I'm not even sure I've come to the right place, but is this the home of Mrs Arthur Rickard?'

'Mrs *Arthur* Rickard?' he said, his eyebrows going further up. 'No, it isn't.'

'Oh dear, I have come to the wrong place,' Clare said, rummaging in her handbag.

'Don't give up so easily. Have another try!'

'I'm afraid I don't understand.'

'I mean, you're almost there. Mrs Rickard does live here. But it's Mrs Miles Rickard, not Mrs Arthur Rickard.'

Clare smiled apologetically. 'It's definitely Mrs Arthur Rickard I'm looking for. I can't think how I came to be given the wrong address. I take it you're Mr Rickard?'

'Then you take it wrong,' the young man said, as though he and Clare were engaged in some parlour game which he was winning rather easily. 'My name's Upton. Now, you're really confused, aren't you?'

'Who is it, Terry?' a woman's voice called out from inside the house. A moment later, a trim, middle-aged blonde appeared at the door. 'Can I be of any help?' she asked, giving Clare a quick appraising look.

'This lady's looking for a Mrs *Arthur* Rickard,' Upton said in a bored tone as though he had suddenly tired of demonstrating his line in repartee. 'I've told her there's no such person living here.'

Pamela Rickard frowned. 'Mrs Arthur Rickard is my husband's mother,' she said. 'She lives at Epsom.'

'I don't see how I could have been expected to know that,' Upton remarked, like a small boy who had just been ticked off. 'I've only met her twice and, as far as I'm concerned, she's Dora.'

His mother ignored him. 'She lives in Credley Road. I don't remember the number, but you'll find it in the telephone book.' She moved to indicate that the doorstep colloquy was at an end. Clare thanked her warmly and nodded to Upton whose expression had now changed from boredom to sulkiness. However, he condescended to give her a wink.

As she walked back along the road, Clare wondered what the second Mrs Rickard offered which the first had lacked. She certainly looked expensive and also gave the impression of being about as tough as polythene wrapping.

It was a quarter to one by the time she reached the bus stop. She had the rest of the day to herself and decided to head for Epsom straight away.

The driver of the bus on the final stage of her journey had no idea where Credley Road was, but suggested she should alight outside the post office.

The telephone directory told her that Mrs Dora Rickard lived at 26 Credley Road and an obliging postman, who pulled up at that moment to empty the letter box, gave her directions how to get there.

The woman who opened the door of number 26 was short with a dumpy figure and hair which seemed to be a different colour depending on which angle of her head you looked at. Nature had contributed grey and light brown and a hairdresser had added two further shades of brown.

'Oh, I'm so glad you're here. Do come in,' she exclaimed and, before Clare could say anything, trotted off into the interior of the house.

Closing the front door, Clare quickly followed her down the hall and to a room which had clearly been added to the house quite recently.

'There they are! I'm afraid the light's not as good as it

51

might be, but I'm so anxious to have your opinion, Miss Wyatt.'

Clare found herself looking at half a dozen pictures hanging on a grey hessian wall. They were obviously Mrs Rickard's own work and now awaited the expert opinion of Miss Wyatt whoever she might be.

'I'm terribly sorry, Mrs Rickard, but I'm not Miss Wyatt.'

'You mean she couldn't come?' The eager expression on Mrs Rickard's face became momentarily dimmed. 'But how nice of you to come in her place,' she said, quickly, brightening. 'Tell me what you think of them, Miss . . . I'm afraid I didn't catch your name.'

'Reynolds. Clare Reynolds. And I haven't called about pictures.'

'You haven't? Well, I don't know what's happened to Miss Wyatt. She was due here an hour ago. Oh dear, I was so looking forward to her coming. You see I met this man who owns a gallery at a party and told him how I had taken up painting and he promised to send along his assistant to look at my pictures. It'd be so exciting to have an exhibition, but I don't suppose they're good enough for that.' She slipped her arm through Clare's in a spontaneous gesture. 'Anyway, you tell me what you think of them? I'm sure you're a good judge.' And she beamed at Clare in such an infectious manner that anything but compliance was out of the question.

For a while, Clare gave her whole attention to the pictures. They were three landscapes, two of them being aspects of the nearby Downs, one of a lake with a boy fishing at the end of a wooden jetty, and three beachscapes with a cold-looking sea and an overcast sky. In one of these, two youths were digging for bait.

'I like them very much,' Clare said. 'I'd have thought that anyone would be pleased to have them hanging on their walls.' Mrs Rickard clapped her hands with delight as Clare went on, 'I particularly like the beachscapes. It seems to me you've caught the air of loneliness and melancholy of a beach in winter.'

'Oh, I'm so glad you like them, Miss Reynolds. Now wait a moment, there's the phone.' She bustled out of the room to return a short time later. 'That was Miss Wyatt. She got held

52

up, she wasn't near a telephone and now she's going to come tomorrow instead.' She came back to where Clare was standing. 'Of course, I've got a lot more, but I picked these out as the ones I'm most pleased with.'

'How long have you been painting?'

'I began about three years ago soon after I moved here. My only son had remarried and I decided to move to a fresh district. My dear husband died six years ago and I've been very much on my own ever since. Not that I've quarrelled with my son, I wouldn't want you to think that, but I don't see very much of him these days. My husband left me provided for and my son runs the business. He's in the motor trade.'

It seemed to Clare as she listened to Mrs Rickard's uninhibited prattle that she was being given all the answers without so much as having to ask the questions. And all this after being ushered into the house as a result of a misunderstanding.

'Have you painted any portraits?' she asked in the lull that followed.

'Not yet. I'd like to try my hand at them, but it's not easy to find anyone willing to sit for hours and days on end.'

'You haven't any grandchildren you could bribe?' Clare said with a smile.

'My son has no children of his own. His second wife has a son, but he's grown up and I've scarcely met him. Anyway, he's a struggling young actor – and I hardly think it would amuse him to sit for me.' She was thoughtful for a moment. 'The idea might flatter him, but that would be all. Between you and me, he's rather a vain young man.' She looked around the room with an abstracted air. Then turning back to Clare, she said, 'Now, Miss Reynolds, let me get you a cup of tea and you can tell me why you called. I'm afraid I've hardly given you a chance to speak.' She giggled. 'The way I pulled you into the house thinking you must be Miss Wyatt. But you took it so well and have been so nice.'

Mrs Rickard was such a disarming person that Clare felt herself considerably less embarrassed than she had reason to. Over the tea, she produced a shorthand notebook and said, 'I really feel rather ashamed admitting it in the circumstances, but I'm one of those awful market researchers. We're trying

53

to find out the extent to which breakfast has declined as a major meal and in what manner.'

'I can answer you in one, my dear,' Mrs Rickard broke in cheerfully. 'All I have is the juice of a freshly squeezed orange, a thin slice of brown bread spread with Bovril and a cup of unsweetened tea. That and nothing else. Seven days a week, fifty-two weeks a year. And you wouldn't think I'll be seventy next year, would you?'

'I can't believe it.'

'Well, I shall be.'

'I'd like to think I'll be as full of life if I ever reach that age,' Clare said with genuine admiration.

Ten minutes later she was on her way back to the bus stop.

That evening when she reported her day's happenings to Nick, he said, 'One can hardly say you have found proof that Dora Rickard is Miles' mother. She might have accepted him as her son in order to save her marriage.'

Clare shook her head. 'I'm convinced she's his true mother.'

'What convinces you?'

'Feminine intuition. The same that, nevertheless, tells me you're right about Stephen Burley.'

CHAPTER NINE

The next evening, as the employees of Rickard Motor Distributors Limited were leaving work, Nick waylaid one of them as she approached her bus stop.

She was a girl called Wendy Smith whom he had met in the course of his enquiries into the burglary. She had been with the company for two years and though Nick had never actually discovered her precise job, it was obvious that she was the senior of the clerks in the general office.

'Hello, Wendy,' he said coming up beside her, 'Can you spare a few moments? Something's cropped up that I'd like your help on.'

'I've got to meet a friend at home in about an hour,' she said in a doubtful tone. 'Is it going to take long?'

'If you give me half an hour, I'll drive you home. I seem to remember you live in Willesden.'

'That's right. It's only fifteen minutes by car.' She glanced about her. 'Where are we going to talk then?'

'Why not in the car? It's parked just over there.'

'You have it all worked out, don't you?' she remarked with a wry smile.

Dodging the traffic they crossed the road and got into Nick's car.

'Before I tell you what it's about,' Nick began, 'I would ask you to treat it as confidential. The reason will become obvious in a moment.' He took a breath. 'I saw Stephen Burley in prison the day before yesterday. He asked me to go as he had something to tell me. He said it was common talk amongst Rickard's employees that Miss Sharman had been old Mr Rickard's mistress and, furthermore, that she was Miles Rickard's true mother. Have you heard that being buzzed around, Wendy?'

'I'm afraid Steve is clutching at straws,' she said. 'There's certainly no question of its being common talk in the office. We had a young clerk called Eric Roberts a few months ago, who overlapped with Steve. He was one of those boys who's not interested in work and he used to spend most of his time interrupting others. He was always starting rumours just for amusement. He once put it out that one of the showroom salesmen had a crush on *me*. I soon told him where he got off. Later, he began this one about Miss Sharman having been the other Mr Rickard's mistress and Mr Miles being their son. Of course, nobody took any notice and shortly after that he left. I mean, even if it were true, how could *he* have known? He just invented things to amuse himself.'

'You yourself don't believe it's true?'

'I certainly wouldn't believe anything put around by Eric Roberts,' she said emphatically. 'Anyway, it's none of my business if Mr Miles' father, who died before I even began working there, was Miss Sharman's lover.' She paused and stared out of the car window. 'I hope the old thing *has* had a lover or two in her life.'

'I gather you like her?'

'I've always got on with her. She has her little ways, but I probably shall have, too, when I'm sixty. She's not sociable with the staff and is apt to play the dragon at the gate if Mr Miles is busy – or she thinks he is – but that's part of her job. She does her best to protect him from intruders. I think that's how Eric Roberts came to start his silly rumour. He got a bit familiar with her one day and she quickly put him in his place.'

'Do you think she would do *anything* to protect Miles?'

'Depends on what you mean by anything, doesn't it?'

'Commit perjury, perhaps?'

She turned her head sharply to see if Nick was being serious.

'Is that the suggestion now?'

'It's certainly Steve Burley's.'

'Oh, well . . . ! He's got an interest in making it, hasn't he?'

'What did you think of *him* when he was working at Rickard's?'

'I liked him. He always struck me as a decent sort of boy. On the quiet side. He was definitely one of the better ones,

56

until . . . until he had that brainstorm.' She looked at Nick with a worried expression. 'I mean, it must have been a brainstorm. I'm sure he'd never have done it otherwise.'

If there was one thing of which Nick was quite certain, it was that a brainstorm had played no part in the matter. He refrained, however, from saying so. Nevertheless, he found it interesting that it was the only way whereby Wendy could rationalise what had happened.

She glanced at her watch. 'We're almost there. I shall be home earlier than usual, thanks to the lift.' She fished a bunch of keys out of her handbag. 'I promise not to tell anyone what we've been talking about. It'd be like lighting a fuse if I did. And I know who the explosion would go off under,' she added with a grin.

'I knew I could rely on your discretion,' Nick said.

'How?' she asked in an intrigued tone.

'Practice. One's constantly having to form judgments of people in the course of an investigation. You soon find out whom you can take into your confidence and whom you can't.'

'Don't you ever make a mistake?'

'From time to time.'

'What do you do then?'

'Cry or curse, depending.' He brought the car to a halt outside the house she indicated. 'Actually, I have one further person I want to ask you about,' he said, as she made a move to get out. 'Miles Rickard.'

'What about him?'

'I'd like to know *your* view of *him*.'

'He's all right,' she said slowly.

'So are fifty million other people. Is he tough, soft, popular with his staff, good-natured, hot-tempered. *What* is he?'

'I think he's basically a nice man, but he's weak in the sense that I doubt whether he stands up to his wife.'

'A lot of men don't.'

'I know. I've always felt that he was probably a womaniser, though he never makes passes at any of the girls in the office. His present wife is tough, all right,' she added as an afterthought.

'Did you ever meet his first wife?'

She shook her head. 'They'd divorced before I began working there.'

'Does the name Wenner mean anything to you?'

'I know who they are, but nothing about them. One or other of them drops by the office occasionally.'

'Yes?' Nick prompted when she seemed about to add something further, but stopped.

'I've had the impression that their visits are not very welcome. Once I bumped into Mr Miles just after the younger one had left and he seemed to be in a state of jitters. Another time one of the showroom salesmen told me he'd heard Mr Miles say something about calling the police and Mr Wenner just laughed. This was when he was seeing him off the premises.' She opened the car door and swung her legs out. 'Thanks again for the ride.' Making a tiny grimace, she added, 'I just hope I haven't already lit that fuse.'

CHAPTER TEN

Miles Rickard stood back from his office window and stared at the retreating back of his visitor as he walked across the forecourt to his car, a dove-grey Rolls new that year.

His gait was relaxed and his rear view, displaying powerful shoulders, reinforced the overall impression of strength.

Rickard clenched his fists tightly in an endeavour to control his emotion; or, more exactly, to stop himself trembling from the mixture of fear and anger which had seized him as soon as Frank Wenner had left his office.

Without a backward glance, Wenner got into his car and drove away. Rickard's eyes followed the faint drift of exhaust smoke until the car was lost from view.

He had just turned back to his desk when Miss Sharman came into the room.

'Your stepson phoned while you were engaged,' she said, 'but I told him you couldn't be disturbed.'

'What did he want?' Rickard asked with a frown.

'He said to tell you he'd done what you wanted with the clothes.'

Rickard's frown grew. 'How dare he phone me in the office about something so . . . so trivial!' he said angrily. Then with a small apologetic smile, he added, 'I'm sorry, Eva, I didn't mean to bite your head off. I'm afraid Frank Wenner's visits always leave me a bit overwrought and my stepson's habit of believing everyone has as much time to waste as he can become a little wearing.'

'He was telling me he hopes to get a part in a new T.V. series,' Miss Sharman remarked. 'He must have quite a lot of talent.'

'*He* certainly thinks so. However, I hope for his sake – as well as for the sake of his mother and myself – that he will get something soon.'

59

Miss Sharman was about to say something further, but checked herself. This was not the moment to unburden her mind, as her employer was obviously not in the mood to listen to other people's worries. Frank Wenner's visit seemed to have provided him with enough of his own. Anyway, she would find an opportunity to talk to him later on.

About half an hour later, he poked his head round the door and said that he was going home for lunch. This in itself was unusual but he vouchsafed no explanation. He didn't return until half past two, by which time the matters requiring his attention had increased in this disrupted day. However, by saying firmly that she would stay late in order to assist him get through his work, Eva Sharman politely blackmailed him into matching her own assiduity. It was nearly seven o'clock when they left the office and he drove her home.

On the way she told him of Clare's visit to her two evenings previously.

'I've several times wished you'd never caught sight of our burglar,' he said with a sigh, 'and then you couldn't have been drawn into all this unpleasantness. I know what an ordeal it was for you going to Court and giving evidence. I wish you could have been spared that.' He paused. 'It's not even that we've recovered any of the money.'

'And with the insurance company refusing to pay . . .'

'That's just tough luck!' he said harshly.

'It's so obvious that it was someone with inside knowledge. No one else would have known that the safe was broken and that cash from sales was kept for a few hours every day in your desk. Only one of the clerks like Stephen Burley would have known.'

'Do you know what I've been thinking, Eva? That Burley wasn't operating alone. I'm sure he'd never have been able to hide the cash without help. Big help. Something Frank Wenner said this morning made me wonder whether he mayn't know something about our burglary.'

'You mean that *he* was behind it?'

Rickard shrugged. 'I've no proof, but . . . but I just wonder.' Noticing Eva Sharman's puzzled look he went on, 'I've not talked to anyone about it, but I think you realise the ruthless person he is. He'll go to any lengths to bend someone to his will and that burglary would be the sort of thing he'd set up in order to do that.'

'So what are you going to do about it?'

'Sleep on it.' He brought the car to a halt outside her home. 'I don't know what'd happen to Rickard's without you, Eva. I sometimes feel that yours is the only sane influence about the place. You're certainly the one indispensible person in the whole outfit.'

'You know there's scarcely anything I wouldn't do for you, Mr Miles.'

Scarcely anything! It was curiously expressed and he pondered it as he drove himself home. But she had always tended to use language cautiously, even sparingly. Her involvement as a witness in the burglary case had, indeed, caused him considerable worry, but she had given a star performance if one could use the theatrical analogy. She had never faltered in her evidence. No one would have stood a chance against the testimony of honest, upright Eva Sharman.

When she brought his mail into his office the next morning, he said immediately, 'I've slept on it and I'm going to tell the police.'

'What exactly are you going to tell them?'

Rickard glanced at his secretary with a faint frown. 'About Wenner of course.'

She had a troubled air as though the night had served only to increase her doubts where it had helped to resolve his.

'If you will get me Sergeant Attwell on the phone, I'll ask him to call round and see me.'

To Nick, the excuse for an official visit to Miles Rickard was unexpectedly welcome and within half an hour he had booked himself out of the station and was on his way.

'Good of you to come round so quickly, sergeant,' Rickard said affably. He walked across to a cupboard in a corner of his office. 'Not too early, is it, to offer you something?' he went on, reaching for a bottle of Scotch.

'Nothing for me, Mr Rickard,' Nick replied firmly.

'Not even a cup of office tea?'

'I'll have that, if it's not a bother.'

'No bother at all. I'll ask Eva to fetch you a cup. Or would you prefer coffee?'

'Yes, coffee please.'

He passed that request via the internal phone on his desk and returned to the cupboard.

'I think I'll have a drop of the hard stuff,' he remarked, pouring himself a sizeable measure of whisky. 'I don't normally drink at this hour of the morning, but that makes the exception more excusable.'

Nick said nothing, but glanced around the office which had become familiar to him in the course of his enquiries into the burglary.

'I hope you've had no further problems with your safe?' he remarked as his eyes alighted on it.

Rickard made a face. 'No, thank God! Though they took long enough to repair it. What a nightmare that whole experience was! I gather that some of Burley's friends are agitating on his behalf. Some woman called on Eva the other evening and asked a lot of impertinent questions, suggesting that Eva might have been wrong in her evidence. Isn't that criminal?'

Nick blinked. 'What, talking to a witness after a case is over?'

'Well, it was more than that. She was almost trying to brainwash Eva.'

'Is that what Miss Sharman says?'

'It's the strong inference I've drawn from what she told me.'

'Would you like me to speak to her about it before I go?' Nick asked a trifle nervously.

'I don't think she wants to take the matter any further, but if any of his friends try that line with me they'll soon get a good thump in their collecting box. Anyway, it's not what I wanted to talk to you about, Mr Attwell.' He stared at the glass in his hand, as though deciding how much to swallow next time he raised it to his lips. Then lifting it, he tossed the lot back. 'Does the name Wenner mean anything to you?'

'I gather that your first wife's name was Wenner,' Nick replied.

'Oh, so you know that, do you?' Rickard remarked in a

tone of faint surprise. He waited for Nick to enlarge upon his reply but when nothing was forthcoming, he went on, 'It's not about my ex-wife that I want to talk, it's about her father and brother, Frank and Alec Wenner. May I take it you've heard of them, too?'

'I know their names,' Nick said warily.

'I imagine you must have quite a dossier on them?'

'What is it you want to tell me about them?' Nick asked, ignoring Rickard's baited hook.

'Well, whether you know it or not, Mr Attwell, you'll find that someone at Scotland Yard knows it. They're a couple of crooks. Big-time boys, the sort who operate at a safe distance and leave those in the front-line to take the raps. My guess is that your bosses at the Yard would give anything for evidence to nail the Wenners.'

'And you have evidence?'

'I hold the key which could provide it.'

Nick noticed that Rickard's hands trembled as he lit a fresh cigarette.

'Am I interesting you?' he went on, squinting at Nick through a mushroom of smoke.

'Go on, I'm listening.'

'About a year ago, the Wenners decided to muscle in on the porn trade, the hard imported stuff. Magazines and films, I don't need to tell *you* the sort of profits that can be made in that line of business. Let's just say that provided you show a bit of sense, it's like printing your own money at home. And the only people who ever get caught are the front-boys, the ones who take the risks. But they get their fines paid for them and if they happen to be put inside for a few months, they're well compensated when they come out again. Occasionally, one of the bigger fish is caught and sent down, but there's always someone to take his place. In a word, Mr Attwell, it's a flourishing trade, despite all the do-gooders and their societies.'

He paused and flicked away some ash which had dropped on to his jacket. Nick remained silent. So far, Rickard had told him nothing of which he was not already aware. There wasn't an officer in the Met Police who did not know how the porn trade thrived.

63

'Anyway, as I say, my ex-father-in-law decided it was high time that he got his share of the profits. Now, the one necessity in that business is good safe, storage space. Somewhere you can keep the stuff, and it often runs into tons, without having to worry about prying eyes. Somewhere the police are unlikely to find it. Are you beginning to get the drift, Mr Attwell?'

'I think so. Wenner wanted to use your premises?'

Rickard nodded. 'There's quite a lot of space at the back. It has a separate entrance and it's reasonably secure. And, of course, it hides behind an innocent car showroom. Perfect! At least that's what Wenner thought until I flatly refused to consider the idea. That was about a year ago. Rather to my surprise he appeared to accept the turn-down, though he did say he thought I'd probably regret the decision. A month or two later he had another go at me with the same result. And then the next thing that happened was the burglary and now, since the trial ended, I've had visits from both Frank and Alec. Alec came a few days ago on what was obviously a softening-up visit and then Frank came yesterday and repeated his demands. He said that, if I didn't co-operate, even nastier things than burglaries could take place.'

'Did he specify?'

'No, but I believe him.' Rickard bit his lip nervously. 'I can't remember whether I told you that my insurance company has refused to pay up. They say that the circumstances of the loss are not covered by my policy. I'm still contesting their decision, but you probably know what it's like fighting an insurance company. They have more tentacles than an octopus.'

'I didn't know about their refusal to pay up,' Nick broke in. 'You certainly never told me.'

'Probably because I was still hoping at the time. Anyway, what difference would it have made?'

'I can't say it would have made any difference, but I ought to have known.'

The truth was that it only assumed significance in Nick's current suspicious frame of mind.

'Well, I'm sorry I forgot to mention it,' Rickard retorted in a faintly huffed tone. 'But to return to the Wenners. I've never got on with either Frank or Alec. Frank was dead against my marrying his daughter and did all he could to prevent it taking place. Perhaps, it's a pity he didn't succeed. During the time we were married, he hardly spoke to me. In fact, he was the main cause of the break-up, for it soon became apparent that he exercised a stronger hold over Helen than I did. After she left me, he became really vindictive and that's been his attitude ever since. If he could break me, he would. What he'd really like is to enmesh me in one of his schemes and then throw me to the wolves.'

Beads of perspiration had formed on Rickard's forehead and his voice had assumed a harsh rasp as he had talked. It was almost as if he expected to hear the wolves massing outside on the forecourt.

'Why have you suddenly decided to disclose this now?' Nick asked.

'Because I believe he may try and do something to damage me.' He glanced quickly round his office. 'It wouldn't be beyond him to cause a fire. He'd know it would be months before I could start up again, even with money from the insurance. If he did try and burn the place down, it wouldn't be past him to start a rumour that I'd done it myself. He's really dangerous, Mr Attwell, when he's on the warpath.' He let out a hollow laugh of despair. 'I realise some of the things you must be thinking, but I can only ask you to believe that it's because I feel myself in danger, I've decided to assist the police in nailing the Wenners. It's not been an easy decision, I can promise you that.'

Nick had realised early on that his own duty would be to inform Tom Tarry of everything Rickard had said and leave the next move to the Serious Crimes Squad. However, he still had his own private investigation to pursue.

'It'll be for my superiors to decide what to do about the information you've supplied, Mr Rickard. As to the possibility of Wenner trying to set fire to your premises, I'll arrange for it to be kept under extra watch at night. Incidentally, you have a man on duty at nights, don't you?'

Rickard shook his head. 'Just visits by a security company. I'd certainly be relieved to think the police were keeping an eye on the place.' He shuddered. 'I don't have to tell you how quickly this lot could go up in flames. Practically everything you look at downstairs is inflammable.'

A few minutes later Nick got up to leave. As he reached the door, he paused and said, 'Oh, by the way, I've got to go and see a Mrs Rickard who lives at Acton in a day or so. Would she be a relative? Your mother, perhaps?'

'I'm not aware of any relatives at Acton. It's certainly not my mother; she lives over at Epsom. There are quite a few Rickards in the telephone book. My father's family originated in Derbyshire. What's happened to Mrs Rickard of Acton?'

'It's an enquiry on behalf of another force,' Nick said, mentally erasing the fictional lady before she could gather further substance.

When he arrived home that evening, he found Clare sitting at the kitchen table with a large pad of paper in front of her and a pencil in hand, both of which had been acquired with a view to encouraging Simon's barely discernible artistic talent.

'Hello, love, what are you scribbling? A new recipe for burnt toast?'

'Another crack like that and it's what you'll get,' she said, offering her face for a kiss. 'As a matter of fact, I've been writing down all we've found out since Burley's conviction.'

'Then let me add to your knowledge.'

When he had finished telling her of his visit to Miles Rickard, she said, 'It's all of a muchness, isn't it, Nick?'

'Meaning?'

'Meaning that we seem to be trudging round the perimeter without getting through to the core.'

Nick nodded. 'And all the while, Stephen Burley languishes in prison.'

He went out of the room and returned with a glass of sherry which he gave to Clare and a bottle of beer for himself.

'There's only one thing for it,' she said after a pensive silence. 'We've got to think of some way of cracking Eva Sharman.'

'Cracking her?' Nick said in a puzzled tone.

'Either cracking her or gaining her confidence, it comes to the same thing. Because until we've done that we're going to *remain* on the perimeter.'

CHAPTER ELEVEN

Normally Eva Sharman had some spring left in her step even at the end of a day's work, but not these last few days. She felt tired and had odd pains, including an endless hovering headache. It had all begun with the visit of that girl who had pretended to be a friend of Stephen Burley's. It had unsettled her more than she wished to admit. And since then there had been other things to increase her sense of disturbance – or, rather, nothing to allay it. It had been like searching for cheerful tidings on the front page of a newspaper and finding none. Everything had confirmed her increasing anxiety and now she was breaking out in physical aches and pains as a direct result of her mental state.

As she turned into her front gate, she let out a soft sigh. At least she was home. Soon she would close the front door on the outside world and busy herself with the small jobs that always awaited her return from work, first of which was always to give Mott a saucer of milk. More often than not he ignored it, but she felt it was an indication to him that he was wanted.

She had scarcely closed the front door behind her when he appeared and began rubbing himself against her legs. She stooped down to stroke him, grateful for his welcome.

'And now I'll get your milk,' she said, moving towards the kitchen.

The cat followed her and watched as she opened her small refrigerator and took out a bottle containing a few inches of milk.

'I'll just add a drop of hot water to take the chill off it,' she said to the observant Mott. But when she placed the saucer down on the floor, he gave it a disdainful sniff and stalked out of the kitchen.

Miss Sharman chuckled. She felt that she and Mott were very much kindred spirits – and she certainly bore him no grudge for his cavalier refusal of her offering. Anyway, she knew that he would drink it later when it suited him.

There was just enough milk left in the bottle for a cup of tea and she put on the kettle.

While she waited for it to boil, she went into the tiny bathroom which led off the kitchen and washed her face and tidied her hair, which made her feel better.

Next she unbolted the door which led from the kitchen into the narrow passage running at the side of the house. It was here that the milkman left her daily pint.

'Oh, it must be a relief man again,' she said in a tone of exasperation as she noticed that the foil top on the bottle had been pecked by a bird. The small plastic yoghurt pot which the delivery man was meant to place on top of the bottle to prevent this happening was still on the step beside the bottle.

Miss Sharman liked birds and was always distressed when Mott caught one, which was not very often, but she did wish he earned his board and lodging by keeping them at bay from her milk. The regular milkman knew what the yoghurt pot was for, but it never seemed to occur to the relief men to place it on top of the bottle and then it was only a matter of time before that impudent little robin flew down and pecked away at the shiny foil top.

Removing what was left of the ragged top, she covered the bottle and put it into the refrigerator.

But when all this was done and she retired into her front room with the cup of tea, it failed to have its usual soothing effect and she found herself again going over recent events in her mind.

Though she fought against admitting it, she knew in her heart of hearts that the moment of crucial decision could not be long deferred. She could not go on bottling up her doubts and fears. She must talk to someone. Her headache became aggravated and she pushed away her tea without finishing it.

After a while she forced herself to get up and draw the curtains. Then she went into the kitchen and washed up her cup and stood wondering what she would have for supper, before deciding that food of any sort was the last thing she wanted.

She returned to her front room and sought solace in her

magazines, but even these failed to divert her mind. She glanced at the paper to see what television offered that evening. A really good thriller might provide the necessary therapy. Best of all would be one of Mr Hitchcock's old films.

But it was one of those nights when the fare on each of the three channels was equally unenticing. A documentary about unmarried mothers, a sports programme and a domestic comedy built round one of the unfunniest men, in Eva Sharman's view, of the whole television age.

Bed seemed to be her only refuge with sleep, if it would come, an always blissful escape from reality.

It took her a little while to convert her living-room into night use. The divan bed had to be pulled out from the wall and the multi-coloured cushions were stacked neatly on a chair. Covers had to be removed and others put on. It was almost a scene-shifter's routine.

When all was ready – and it seemed to take longer than usual on this particular evening – she undressed with the same fastidious care, folding her clothes and laying them neatly on a chair. Then she went into the kitchen and made herself a bedtime drink of hot chocolate for which she used the fresh bottle of milk.

Finally, she was ready for bed and slid gratefully into its womb-like comfort. She reached for her sleeping pills and gazed thoughtfully for a moment at the bottle. Small pink capsules which could calm the turmoil of her mind.

She washed the capsules down and drained her cup of chocolate.

Then she switched off the light and lay back . . . and waited.

Soon she had a most peculiar sensation. It was as if her mind and body had been wrenched apart and she was watching her body rapidly change shape like a cartoon creation. A coloured cartoon because her body – or what had once looked like a body – was reflecting bright fluorescent colours.

It really was most peculiar, though not wholly unpleasant and not a bit alarming.

But peculiar . . . oh, so peculiar.

CHAPTER TWELVE

'Have you seen Eva, Wendy?' Miles Rickard's tone was worried.

Wendy Smith looked up from her typewriter to find her employer standing in the doorway of the clerks' room.

'No, Mr Rickard? Isn't she in yet?'

Wendy's own tone was one of surprise as normally you could set your watch by Eva Sharman's arrival.

Rickard shook his head. 'I wondered whether you might have had a message. It's unlike her to be late without warning somebody.'

'She could have got held up in a traffic jam or perhaps her bus has gone on strike. Would you like me to sort your mail and look after things until she comes? She'll probably turn up in the next half hour.'

'I'd be grateful if you would, Wendy.'

But half an hour later she still hadn't arrived, nor had there been any message to explain her absence.

'The trouble is she's not on the phone so we can't call her,' Rickard said. 'I can't think what can have happened.'

'Would you like me to go round to her house?' Wendy asked. 'If I could take a car, I'll be there and back inside of half an hour.'

'I think I ought to go myself, but I'll be glad if you'll come with me.' He shook his head in a worried fashion. 'She's been with us for thirty years and this is the first time I can recall her failing to arrive without some explanation.'

'Of course, if she's been taken ill and doesn't have a phone, it's not easy for her to get a message through.'

'But she's never ill,' Rickard exclaimed. 'Apart from a winter cold which doesn't keep her away, she's not had a day's illness all the time she's worked here.'

'She's over sixty, Mr Rickard,' Wendy said firmly, 'and people of that age can and do fall ill without warning.' What she really meant was 'fall dead', but hadn't liked to say so quite as bluntly.

As they drew up outside the house where Eva Sharman lived, they both peered anxiously at the drawn curtains over the front window.

'That's her room,' Rickard said with a catch in his voice.

He led the way to the front door and put his finger hard on the bell push. No sound of movement came from within and he resorted to the knocker. Meanwhile, Wendy shaded her eyes and tried to peer round the side of the drawn curtains, but was unable to see into the room.

With Rickard still knocking and ringing, she moved to the other side of the front door where the narrow passage ran down the short length of the house.

'I'll try this other door,' she announced and disappeared down the passage. A moment or two later Rickard joined her.

She pressed her face against the kitchen window, but suddenly jumped back with a small scream as Mott leapt nimbly on to the sill on the inside and they came face to face through the pane of glass.

'I wish you hadn't done that,' she said reproachfully while Mott merely gave her a yellow stare.

She had hardly recovered when there was a rattle of milk bottles and the milkman appeared at the other end of the passage. He halted in his tracks and stared at them suspiciously.

'We're from Miss Sharman's place of work,' Wendy said. 'She didn't turn up this morning and we've come round to see if anything's wrong. This is Mr Rickard, her employer.'

'Doesn't she answer then?' the milkman asked, coming down the passage to where they were standing. 'Anyway, her cat's all right,' he remarked as he caught sight of Mott through the window. 'Of course, I only sees her on Saturdays when she pays me for her week's milk. Ordinary, I just leaves her pint on the step, remembering,' he went on with a grin, 'to put that little pot over it. Otherwise the birds peck off the top and she don't like that.'

He had matched action to his words as he spoke and he

71

now picked up the empty bottle which had been on the step and put it in his crate.

'If you want to get in, I reckon you'd best force that window,' he said pointing to one on the further side of the door. 'It's only got one of them flimsy catches. Hope nothing's happened to the old girl.' He paused in the act of departure. 'Leave a note if she doesn't need no more milk.'

'I'll go and fetch a tyre lever from the car,' Rickard said grimly. 'I think that probably is the easiest window to force.'

While he was gone, Wendy took a further look into the kitchen, unembarrassed by Mott who had disappeared. It looked as neat and tidy as she would have expected. There wasn't an unwashed cup or plate in sight.

Rickard returned carrying the tyre lever. 'You'd better stand back a bit,' he said, inserting one end half way up the window near the catch. 'Something may fly off.'

In the event the pane of glass cracked as the window burst open, but that and a mis-shapen catch was the sum of the damage.

'I'll climb in and unlock the door,' Rickard said nervously.

A minute later, Wendy had joined him inside the kitchen. They stared at each other for a second of frozen silence, then Rickard led the way through the half-open kitchen door into the hall.

On their right was the door of her room. It was ajar and Rickard cocked an ear to the opening.

'Miss Sharman,' he called out.

There was a soft movement inside and Mott appeared round the edge of the door. He rubbed himself against Wendy's legs and proceeded into the kitchen.

Cautiously Rickard pushed the door open and switched on the light.

The sight which met their gaze was one of disorder. The bedclothes were strewn about the room and items of clothing were similarly scattered, one stocking dangling from the lampshade which hung in the middle of the room.

At the foot of the bed an arm and a leg protruded from a tangle of blankets.

'Oh my God!' Rickard said and swallowed hard.

He moved further into the room and pulled back part of a

72

blanket so that the back of Eva Sharman's head came into view. Her face was pressed against the floor as though she had been trying to burrow into the ground.

'Don't touch anything,' Wendy hissed in a tone of frozen horror.

But she had no need to have spoken for Rickard hurriedly pushed past her as he made a dash from the room. A second later she heard him being violently sick.

CHAPTER THIRTEEN

Nick was immersed in paperwork when he received a summons to accompany Detective Chief Superintendent Rudgwick to the scene of a suspicious death.

'It's that woman who was a witness in your Old Bailey case,' Rudgwick said, as Nick joined him in the waiting car.

'Eva Sharman?' Nick exclaimed in astonishment.

Rudgwick nodded. 'Dead on her bedroom floor. Room in disorder, but no obvious cause of death.' He paused and added as an afterthought, 'Could be heart failure grappling with an intruder, I suppose. That'd still be manslaughter.'

'Who found her?'

'I gather someone went round to her house when she failed to turn up at work this morning.'

Ten minutes later their car pulled up behind two others parked outside her home. The front one was a police car with its blue roof light revolving and its radio crackling with staccato messages. A number of bystanders stood staring at a scene made familiar on television.

'Can't you switch that thing off?' Rudgwick asked, addressing the driver who was the sole occupant of the police car. The man blinked. 'The thing on your roof,' Rudgwick added impatiently. 'It only draws crowds.'

'And who might you be?' the officer enquired with hostility.

'Tell him, Nick,' Rudgwick said and strode up to the front door.

'Detective Chief Superintendent Rudgwick,' Nick said to the now puzzled-looking constable.

It seemed to Nick that the man was about to argue the toss, but with a shrug he leaned forward and moved a switch. Nick hurried after Rudgwick, reflecting that there were still sensitive areas of demarcation between the uniformed and C.I.D. branches.

He arrived in the narrow hall to find Rudgwick speaking to the local police surgeon, Dr Fison.

'I'd say she's been dead at least twelve hours,' Dr Fison said. 'I've not moved her more than I had to, as the photographer hasn't arrived yet, but I can't see any external injuries. There are some sleeping tablets on her bedside table and a cup with dregs of a sort in it which you'll obviously want to preserve for analysis.'

'Let's take a look,' Rudgwick remarked stepping inside the room, followed by Dr Fison and Nick.

The scene was macabre enough, but to Nick even more so when he reflected that this was the neat, tidy room in which Clare had sat and talked to Eva Sharman a few days previously.

Rudgwick propounded the tentative theory he had mentioned to Nick in the car. Dr Fison nodded judiciously.

'That's certainly a possibility,' he said. 'Though I'm told there's no sign of a forcible entry which seems to rule out an intruder.'

'He might have gained legitimate entry.'

Dr Fison gave Rudgwick a quizzical look. 'I would not have expected a lady of Miss Sharman's years to have entertained in her night attire. But that's your province, not mine.' He glanced at his watch. 'If there's nothing else I'll be on my way. I was in the middle of my morning rounds when I was called here. Who'll be doing the autopsy, as I'd be interested to be present?'

'I'll speak to the coroner right away. I expect it'll be Professor Travers if he's available.'

A uniformed sergeant was in the hall as they emerged from the bedroom.

'Sergeant Hill, sir,' he announced smartly. 'I have Mr Rickard and the lady's cat in the kitchen, sir. It was Mr Rickard who discovered what had happened and sent for the police. We were on patrol in the vicinity and were directed here. I reported my initial findings, sir, and photographic and fingerprint people are on their way.'

'Fine, sergeant. I'd like to go and use the radio in your car. By the way, what's the name of your driver?'

'Constable Beddington, sir. Any reason for asking, sir?' His tone was suspicious.

'No. I just wondered, that's all.'

'I'll come with you, sir.'

Rudgwick turned to Nick. 'You better go and talk to Rickard.' He frowned and turned back to Sergeant Hill. 'Any reason for detaining the cat?' he enquired in a puzzled tone.

'I thought it better to do so, sir, in the interests of preserving the scene. An examination of its coat might reveal a clue.' And then as though to head off any criticism he added, 'I've allowed it to be given food. Cat food from its own tin. But I've instructed that nothing else in the kitchen should be touched.'

'You've done very well, sergeant,' Rudgwick remarked, reflecting that the days were now happily past when the first officers at the scene of a crime left it looking as though a herd of elephants had been staging a reunion. There could still be unfortunate mishaps, but they were much less frequent than when he began life in the police.

As Rudgwick followed Sergeant Hill out to the car, Nick went into the kitchen to find its three occupants in various attitudes of gloomy silence.

Rickard was sitting slumped on the only chair with a blank expression. Leaning against the outside door was a young P.C. with arms folded across his chest and sitting on the sill staring out of the window was Mott, his back a formidable reproach to the kitchen and everyone in it.

'Hello, Mr Attwell,' Rickard said, with the obvious relief of someone seeing a familiar face. 'I can't believe it's happened. Poor Eva! You've heard how Wendy Smith and I found her?'

'I'd like to hear it from you,' Nick said. 'Incidentally, where is Wendy?'

'The sergeant said she could leave and she's gone back in my car.' He then described in detail their arrival at the house, the break-in and their discovery of Eva Sharman's body. 'What on earth can have happened?' he asked at the end, giving Nick an anguished look.

'We shan't know that until her cause of death has been established. But it must be either suicide or murder. Well, anyway homicide,' he added recalling Rudgwick's tentative theory.

'But why should she have committed suicide?'

'That's something the police'll be asking you if it turns out that way.'

'She didn't seem to have been quite her usual self the last few days, but she'd be the last person to have taken her own life. I was only saying to her a day or two ago that she provided the one *sane* element in our company.'

'One never knows what's going on in other people's minds,' Nick replied, opening the small refrigerator and peering inside. The contents were sparse. A small amount of butter, four eggs, a packet of bacon and two bottles of milk, one full, the other only half-full.

'That full bottle was delivered this morning while we were trying to get in,' Rickard said. 'Wendy put it in the fridge.'

Nick nodded and closed the door of the refrigerator.

'I suppose you'll want me to make a statement, Mr Attwell?'

'Certainly. And Wendy, too.'

'I expect you can guess what I'm thinking?'

'Whether the Wenners put any pressure on Miss Sharman?'

'Whether they murdered her, Mr Attwell,' he said, his eyes mirroring a mixture of horror and loathing.

Nick said nothing. He didn't know whether Eva Sharman had committed suicide or whether she had been murdered. Time would reveal. But what he already felt certain of was that her death was in some way connected with the burglary and Stephen Burley.

CHAPTER FOURTEEN

Rudgwick came into the kitchen while Nick was still there.

'This is Mr Rickard,' Nick said, introducing him to Eva Sharman's employer.

'She'd worked for you a long time, I gather?' Rudgwick remarked, shaking Rickard's hand.

'Over thirty years. She was originally my father's secretary.'

Rudgwick nodded in an abstracted way as he gazed about him.

'Sergeant Attwell's doubtless told you the form. We can't get very far until her cause of death has been determined. If it's suicide, the coroner will expect to have some indication of a motive. Suicides usually leave notes explaining why they've decided to kill themselves. Of course, there may be one somewhere, though it's not in any obvious place. But her room's in such a mess, one can't yet say for certain. Once the pathologist and the various other experts have been and done what they have to, we'll check it right through.'

'Mr Rickard is convinced that Miss Sharman would never have committed suicide,' Nick said.

'Maybe he's right,' Rudgwick observed. He glanced across at Mott who was still staring out of the window. 'Is that the clue-carrying cat Sergeant Hill mentioned?' he enquired. Nick nodded and Rudgwick went over and gently scratched the top of Mott's head. 'Wonder what you could tell us, cat, if you were able to talk.'

Mott craned his head up for further attention, but Rudgwick turned away.

'No point in our keeping Mr Rickard here, Nick. Take him back in my car and have a good look round Miss Sharman's office while you're there. Then come back here.'

The throng of curious bystanders had grown when Nick and Rickard emerged from the house and were being kept at a distance by officers who had been despatched from the local police station for crowd and traffic control.

A press photographer dashed into the road as the car drew away and a flashlight exploded on the side Rickard was sitting. He jerked away from the window in momentary alarm.

'What the hell was that?' he asked angrily.

'Press photographer. Probably hoped to see you in handcuffs,' Nick said. 'Though he ought to have known that you'd have had a blanket over your head if you were as interesting as that.'

Rickard straightened himself in his seat. 'I hope you'll make it clear to my staff that I'm not under arrest,' he said in a tense voice.

When they arrived outside Rickard Motor Distributors Limited, Nick let Rickard get out first and then allowed a few seconds to elapse before he emerged from the car himself. Even then, he paused and shook one leg of his trousers before sauntering after Rickard who by this time was already entering the building. He was aware of eyes following him as he walked through the showroom and up the flight of stairs at the rear which led to the first floor office.

Rickard was standing outside the door of Eva Sharman's office when Nick reached the top of the stairs.

'I don't know where you want to start,' he said when he had closed the door behind them.

Frankly, Nick didn't want to start anywhere under Miles Rickard's watchful eye, but he could hardly tell the owner of the place to remove himself.

'I'd like to look through these drawers,' he said, perching himself on the typist's swivel chair behind the desk.

There were four drawers on one side and one large one on the other. He opened the big one first and saw that it comprised a small cabinet of files. Their neatly labelled spines faced upwards and bore such legends as, 'M.R: personal insurance', 'M.R: petty cash receipts' and 'M.R: misc. correspondence.'

'M.R. is you, I assume?' Nick said.

'Yes. She kept all files relating to my personal affairs here.'

It seemed unlikely that Eva Sharman, if she had left any

note behind, would have secreted it in any of the files relating to her employer's business.

Nick turned his attention to the four drawers on the other side. The top one contained a stock of the firm's note paper and envelopes. The next one had carbon paper and boxes of paper clips and rubber bands, also a selection of coloured pens in a glass tray. The third was full of items for her typewriter. Spare ribbons, a number of small brushes and a curious looking metal tool.

The bottom drawer was locked and Nick threw Rickard a questioning look.

'You'll find the key on a hook at the back of the top drawer,' Rickard said. 'It's only locked because it's the drawer in which she kept the petty cash and the stamps.' His tone seemed deliberately deflationary.

Nick opened the drawer and peered at the contents. There was, indeed, a small black metal cash box and beneath it an unmarked buff folder.

'What's this contain?' he asked, lifting out the folder.

Rickard frowned. Was it Nick's imagination or did he also look suddenly anxious?

'I've no idea,' he said in a tight voice, watching intently as Nick opened it.

Nick recognised the top piece of paper immediately as a typed copy of Eva Sharman's witness statement relating to the burglary. She had asked to be given a copy before the trial and he had supplied it, telling her that she wouldn't, however, be allowed to refer to it when she was giving her evidence.

Clipped to it were three sheets of pencilled notes which Nick recalled having seen when he took the statement from her. She had explained how she had come to make them within half an hour of the burglary taking place for fear that delayed shock might bring a distortion of her recollection of events. He now recalled having commended her, adding that he wished all the witnesses with whom he had to deal were as meticulous.

He glanced quickly at the pages of notes, his eye caught by a number of heavily underlined sentences.

'Saw his scar quite clearly.'

'No doubt at all it was Stephen Burley.'

'No mistaking his scar.'

Nick became aware that Rickard had moved closer to the desk in order to see better the contents of the folder. At the same time his attention was riveted by a plain sheet of paper which was detached from the others. It also bore pencilled writing, but it was a name which caused Nick to stifle quickly the gasp that came to his lips. Clare's name.

'Hardly home yesterday evening,' he read, 'when a woman who said her name was Clare Reynolds arrived at the door. Having inveigled me into conversation about Mott, she disclosed that she was a friend of Stephen Burley's fiancée. She then tried to get me to admit that I might have made a mistake in my identification. She said that all his friends were convinced of his innocence. When I made it clear that I was not prepared to discuss the case with her in detail she left.

I wonder who she really was. There are so many snoopers around these days. But I found her visit disturbing. I am writing these notes the next day, but still feel unsettled by her suggestion.

I spoke to M.R. the day after, but he was preoccupied with other matters. I am still bothered. More than ever. Must speak to M.R. again.'

And there the notes ended towards the bottom of the page. Whatever the reason, the record was incomplete.

Rickard, who had been frustrated in his effort to read it upside down when Nick had held it so that he couldn't see the writing, stood watching with a smouldering expression.

'You told me yesterday when I was here that Miss Sharman had mentioned a visit from someone who said she was a friend of Burley's fiancée?'

'That's right, she did,' Rickard said, in a tone designed to indicate his continuing sense of affront.

'Did she ever mention the matter to you a second time?'

'Not that I recall.'

'Well, you would recall, wouldn't you?'

'She never brought the subject up again. I'm quite sure about that. Why?'

81

'Because, according to this note, she intended to do so.'

'She didn't.'

'I should like to take this folder with me, Mr Rickard.'

'I don't suppose I can stop you,' Rickard said bleakly.

'I'm sure you wouldn't wish to if it'll help unravel the mystery of Miss Sharman's death.'

He thought that Rickard was about to ask if he might read the notes when there was a knock on the door and Wendy Smith announced that there was someone who wished to speak to him urgently in the showroom.

Nick heaved a small sigh of relief. He preferred Rickard not to see the document, but would have found it difficult to give him a blank refusal.

'Isn't it terrible about Miss Sharman?' Wendy said, with a catch in her voice.

'It must have been a horrible shock when you found her,' Nick remarked.

'Thank goodness there were two of us. I'd have passed out if I'd been on my own.'

'That's understandable. Tell me, Wendy, do you have any idea why Miss Sharman might have committed suicide?'

'So it was suicide?'

'We don't know yet. But supposing it was, can you think why?'

Wendy gazed past Nick with a thoughtful expression. 'Not really, unless it's what you said in the car the other evening.' Noticing Nick's puzzled frown, she added, 'You suggested she might have committed perjury at Steve's trial.'

'I gathered then you didn't agree.'

'Frankly, I don't know what to think any more. It's all much deeper than it seemed.'

'Wheels within wheels, you mean?'

'Sort of, yes.'

'You haven't heard anything since we spoke?'

'No. Nor have I breathed a word to anyone about what we discussed.'

'Good girl! But go on keeping your ears and eyes open. I must get back to Miss Sharman's. Will you tell Mr Rickard I'll be in touch with him later in the day?'

Deciding that he would avoid running the gauntlet of the

showroom, Nick went down the other staircase and let himself out of the pavement door at the bottom, pulling it locked behind him.

Rudgwick's driver was a taciturn officer of the old school who had never achieved promotion, but who was perfectly content driving a Detective Chief Superintendent around the metropolis. His name was Harry and he never grumbled at the long hours or the tedious waits. Above all, he never spoke unless spoken to and it was impossible ever to know what he was thinking.

All this suited Nick who had some intensive thinking of his own to do on the return journey. The folder containing Eva Sharman's notes lay on his lap. They were clearly relevant to the investigation of her death and it was his duty to show them to Rudgwick. If only they didn't mention Clare by name. But they did; moreover, in a way to excite the interest of any conscientious investigating officer. Rudgwick would certainly want to know more about Clare Reynolds. Who was she? What was she up to? If Nick said nothing, it wouldn't take Rudgwick very long to discover that she was Mrs Nick Attwell and then there really would be some explaining to do. Silence might postpone the day of explanation, but it would make it a very much more daunting one when it did arrive. No, there was only one thing for it, he would have to tell Rudgwick of Clare's activities when he showed him the notes. And that would mean also explaining his private doubts about Burley's conviction. But perhaps Eva Sharman's death converted them from private to official doubts and it was now his duty to declare them anyway. If he could hold off doing anything until tomorrow, he could then discuss it with Clare.

The car pulled up outside the house. There were now several others parked at the kerb and the throng of bystanders seemed to remain at a constant strength. As one drifted away, he was replaced by a fresh face wanting to know what had happened.

Nick hurried into the house which now seemed to be bursting with people. Rudgwick stood in the doorway of the front room talking to a small, wiry man with a shock of springy red hair whom Nick recognised as Professor Travers, the pathologist. He gave the impression of a small bright-eyed dog impatiently waiting to be let off the lead.

Inside the room was one of the civilian photographers from Scotland Yard who was just getting ready to leave and an officer of the fingerprint section.

'This is Detective Sergeant Attwell, professor,' Rudgwick said.

'Won't shake hands,' Travers said, holding up his hands so that Nick could see they were encased in transparent polythene gloves. 'Just about to start work.' He looked across at the fingerprints officer. 'How much longer is that fellow going to be?'

'Give me a couple of minutes, sir, and I'll be out of your way,' the officer in question called out without looking round.

'Don't you go!' Travers said as the photographer pushed past him at the door. 'There'll be more work for you once I'm allowed in.'

'I'm *not* going,' the photographer replied tartly, rolling his eyes at Nick. If the pathologist wasn't careful, he would take a photo of *him* in some unbecoming position.

Rudgwick turned to Nick. 'The flat above's empty,' he said. 'A Mrs Hutchings lives there. She's a widow, but she's gone away to stay with her married daughter, so that line of enquiry didn't get us very far. The people who live in the house that side' – he nodded his head at the farther wall of Eva Sharman's room – 'are a Mr and Mrs Elcolino. Mr Elcolino is deaf and Mrs Elcolino suffers from her nerves, but she thought she heard sounds coming from this room quite early in the evening. About eight o'clock. She describes them as bumps. There were no screams and she didn't hear any voices. She would, however, normally only hear raised voices, she says.' He gave Nick a resigned shrug. 'I've sent Perkins and Baskomb knocking on other friendly neighbourhood doors,' he added, 'but more for something to do than in any hope. Everything's going to depend on what he tells us.' As he moved in to watch, he nodded at Professor Travers who was now kneeling beside the body.

Nick, too, drew closer as the pathologist carefully turned Eva Sharman over on to her back. Her eyes were shut but her mouth was open with the lips drawn back in a grimace. Nick shivered and averted his gaze, but as quickly forced himself to look down again. It was always worse when the body was of someone you had known in life.

It was several minutes before Professor Travers straightened up.

'Not a sign of external injury,' he announced. 'Of course, I'll take a much closer look at the mortuary, particularly for puncture marks of the skin and the like.' He got to his feet, but continued to stare down at the body. 'No smell, no sign of vomit,' he went on in a musing tone, 'no obstruction of the mouth.' He let his glance roam round the room. 'But all this disorder. Rather puzzling – and that's not a comment you often hear from me.'

'The disorder and her death may be differently related,' Rudgwick observed.

Professor Travers nodded. 'I confess that hadn't occurred to me, but it could be so. An intruder creates the disorder searching for something in her room, in the course of which the old lady suffers a heart attack brought on by stress and dies. Yes, that would certainly account for the scene as we now find it. But *did* the old lady have a heart attack?' He looked at Rudgwick with his head on one side. 'That's something I'll be able to tell you very soon.'

Stepping lightly over the body, he went to the bedside table and sniffed at the cup containing the dregs of her bedtime drink. Next he examined the bottle of sleeping tablets.

'Only four left,' he murmured.

'Wouldn't you have expected her to have vomited if she'd taken an overdose?' Rudgwick enquired.

'In the normal way, yes. But if it was only a small overdose, no.'

'But would a small overdose have killed her?'

'If her heart was in poor shape, it could have done.'

'I gather she was remarkably healthy,' Nick remarked. 'Never had a day off on account of illness.'

'You can be a few heart-beats away from death and be in blissful ignorance of the fact,' Professor Travers said breezily. 'Providence doesn't give each of us the same amount of warning, you know.'

Nick met the dancing glint in his eyes with a stony stare.

85

'You'll be sending these bits and pieces to the lab?' the pathologist asked, looking across at Rudgwick.

'I want *everything* got ready for submission to the lab,' Rudgwick said firmly. 'I'm not taking any chances until we have a definite line of enquiry.'

'Wise man, wise man,' Professor Travers murmured, taking a final look round the room. 'I'll see you at the mortuary.' He paused at the door and glanced back once more. 'Puzzling. All that disorder and not a sign of injury. Distinctly puzzling.'

A few minutes later, Eva Sharman's body, covered by a sheet, had been carried out on a stretcher to the waiting ambulance and driven away to the mortuary, followed by the Yard photographer in his car who had not, after all, been required to take any further photographs in the house.

Rudgwick and Nick were about to leave when Sergeant Hill came in and said that there were several reporters outside and would Detective Chief Superintendent Rudgwick please speak to them.

There were four of them by the front gate as Rudgwick and Nick emerged from the house.

'Is it murder?' one of them called out.

'I'm afraid I can't tell you what it is, because we don't know.'

'But it could be murder?'

'It could be murder, it could be suicide. All I can tell you is that a woman has died in suspicious circumstances and, for the time being, the police are keeping an open mind.'

'If it's murder, do you have a suspect in mind?'

'That's a hypothetical question and I never answer them.'

'Do you agree that it's a bit of a coincidence that this has happened just after she was a vital witness in one of your cases at the Old Bailey?'

Nick realised that the questioner was looking at him, but before he could answer, Rudgwick said, 'The police don't speculate about coincidences.' With a toothy grin he added, 'Not out loud and in front of the press, anyway.'

But as he and Nick drove off in his car, he said, 'Well, *is* it only a coincidence that sudden death has overtaken Miss Sharman so soon after giving evidence?'

CHAPTER FIFTEEN

Clare jumped down off the chair on which she had been standing and removed the scarf which covered her head.

Standing back she surveyed her handiwork. On the whole she thought she had made a good job. She didn't expect to receive Simon's praise when he returned home, for it was unlikely that he would even notice that his bedroom walls had been transformed from off-white – very off, in fact – to primrose yellow. But at least she was pleased with the result.

When Nick had phoned half way through the day to tell her of Eva Sharman's death and to say he wouldn't be back till late, she had been left at a loose end. Deprived of her son's lively company and with no further line of enquiry to pursue, she had resorted to repainting his small bedroom. For once she seemed to have got rather less paint over herself. Nevertheless she decided to have a bath before starting to prepare supper. Her watch told her it was only eight o'clock and Nick would not be home for at least another hour.

She was just about to go into the bathroom when she heard a key turn in the front door and Nick came in.

'I'm home, darling,' he called out.

Clare looked down at him from the top of the stairs.

'I was about to take a bath,' she said.

'Can't we have supper first, I'm famished.'

'I'm reeking of paint.'

'I don't mind. You can reek of anything and I'll still love you.'

'I must remember that.'

'Anyway, what have you been painting?'

'Simon's room. Come and see.'

Nick bounded up the stairs, kissing Clare warmly when he reached the top.

'Not a bad flavoured paint,' he remarked, licking his lips

87

and looking through the door of Simon's room. 'Great job, darling! Now let's have supper.'

'I'd have had it ready,' Clare said defensively, 'if you'd told me you were going to be back by eight.'

'Eight! It's nearer ruddy half past nine.'

Clare studied her watch again, frowned and gave it a shake. 'It must have stopped.'

'You've got paint in it,' Nick remarked, leading her firmly into the kitchen. 'Just let me get a beer and then I'll tell you everything that's happened. Sherry for you?'

He began by telling Clare of his finding the notes left by Eva Sharman in which she referred to Clare's visit.

'I'd hoped not to have to do anything about them until I'd been able to discuss the position with you, darling,' he said watching her as she moved from food cupboard to stove to refrigerator.

'But it didn't work out that way?' she asked, giving him a faintly anxious look.

He shook his head. 'Old Rudgwick wanted to know if I'd found anything in her office which bore on her death and I was obliged to show him the folder of papers I'd taken possession of.'

'What was his reaction?'

'He asked me point blank if I had any idea who Clare Reynolds was?' Nick said with a rueful grin. 'So what could I say?'

'What *did* you say?' Clare had paused, pan in hand, and was looking apprehensively at her husband.

'I said she was better known to me as Mrs Attwell. Then, of course, I had to tell him the whole story, of my uneasiness about Burley's conviction and of my . . . our nosing around to see if there was any substance to it.'

'Poor love!' Clare exclaimed. 'It must have been like entering the fiery furnace.'

'It was a bit, though, as luck would have it, I turned out to be the guy who didn't get burnt. Well, not yet.'

'Where did luck come into it?'

'Rudgwick took the view that the burglary, Eva Sharman's death and the Wenner connection were more than likely part of the same picture. At any rate he was disposed to believe that until the contrary was proved. And that meant he accepted my concern about Burley's conviction as being possibly well-founded.' Nick paused and took a swig of beer. 'Don't run away with the idea that he gave me a round of applause, but at least he didn't tear me apart. In fact, what he did say was that he would reserve judgment until events proved me right or wrong.'

'Sentence postponed,' Clare remarked, turning back to the stove. 'Did he say anything about my part?'

'Yes.' When Nick didn't go on, Clare looked round to see him grinning at her. 'What he said was, "I don't know why your missus doesn't rejoin the force, seeing what she gets up to, unpaid." '

Clare let out a laugh. 'He's got a point.' She switched her attention back to what she was cooking. 'Tell me about Eva Sharman's death. What did the p.m. show?'

'Professor Travers says that she died of heart failure, but what caused it is still a mystery. She'd taken sleeping tablets, but not in such quantity as to produce the normal signs of a massive overdose. On the other hand, Travers says that even a minor overdose could have killed her if her heart had been in a poor state.'

'But he finds no evidence that it was?' Clare broke in.

'Exactly.'

'No sign of any injuries.'

'None, neither external nor internal. There was some oedema of the brain which he couldn't account for. But that was all.'

'That's swelling, isn't it?'

Nick nodded. 'So the upshot is that all her organs have got to be separately examined in the laboratory and those tests can take time.'

'Meanwhile you don't know whether you have a murder, a suicide or an accidental death on your hands?' Clare's expression showed that she had suddenly thought of something. 'Did the p.m. reveal whether she'd ever given birth to children?' she asked eagerly.

'She was still virgo intacta,' Nick replied.

'That puts an end to that particular trail.'

89

'It also confirms your intuition,' he said with an affectionate smile.

A silence fell as he watched her take the lamb chops from under the grill and then drain the beans.

'If you can emerge from your reverie,' she said, 'we can start eating.'

'The most puzzling feature,' he said a few minutes later, as he cut off a lump of meat and put it thoughtfully into his mouth, 'was the disorder in her room. It wasn't just the tangle of sheets and blankets on the floor, but bits of her own clothing scattered around as though she had thrown everything into the air and let it fall at random. Why should she have done that, Clare?'

'If there was swelling of her brain, may she not have done it while in a state of frenzy?'

'In that event, Professor Travers says he'd have expected to find she'd injured herself. But there wasn't a mark or a bruise on her.'

'Then the disorder must have been caused by someone else.'

'That's the guvnor's theory at the moment. But who and what was he doing?'

'Obviously searching for something. And at some stage after his entry, Miss Sharman has a heart attack and dies. Presumably before the disorder. Afterwards because she's dead, he doesn't bother to tidy the place. Presumably because he's in a hurry to get away.'

'There was no sign of a break-in,' Nick said.

'Because whoever it was had a key.'

Nick laid down his knife and fork and let out a satisfied sigh.

'It all seems a very long way from Stephen Burley and a burglary,' he observed in a reflective tone.

Reaching for his plate, Clare said, 'Distances can be very deceptive.'

CHAPTER SIXTEEN

When Alec Wenner arrived at the breakfast table the next morning, his father, who, as usual, had long finished his own, pushed a copy of a newspaper across the table, indicating a paragraph on the folded page with a stubby but well manicured finger.

He said nothing but watched his son as he read it while continuing to spoon cereal into his mouth. 'It's lucky you don't need your mouth for reading,' he remarked, unbottling some of the exasperation Alec aroused in him at breakfast time.

'If I did, this'd have to wait,' Alec replied, looking up from the paper while still eating.

'Get on, read it.'

'I've read it. "Mysterious death of sixty-two-year-old spinster." '

'I don't mean read it to me.'

'What *do* you mean? All that pounding you give your old body when sensible folk are still in bed doesn't make you any better company at breakfast. Hey, Helen, I'm ready for my bacon and eggs.'

His sister appeared with a plate and put it before him, removing his empty cereal bowl.

'If you go on indulging the way you do, you won't be anyone's company by the time you're my age, because you won't get to my age. You'll be dead long before then.'

'Like poor old Eva Sharman, eh!' He gave his father an amused grin. 'How long are we going to give Rickard, Frank, before we find out whether he's got a bit of sense at last?'

'A day or so.'

'And if he hasn't, then . . .' Alec Wenner made a gesture suggestive of wringing out a towel.

'It may need a bit of finesse. We don't want him breaking and rushing off to the police with tears in his eyes.'

'I'm all for breaking him. Isn't that precisely what we want to achieve?'

'It's a squeezing, not a breaking, operation.'

'Same thing to me.'

'You'll never learn finesse, will you?'

'O.K., so we've squeezed and now we sit back and wait.'

'I've said, for a day or so.'

'And then we squeeze again?'

'If it's necessary.'

Alec Wenner broke off a piece of bread and put it on the end of his fork to mop up the residue of egg on his plate.

'If you ask me, you can have too much bloody finesse,' he remarked.

'Watch your tongue! You know the old lady wouldn't have that word in the house. Anyway, what d'you mean, too much finesse?'

'What I mean, Frank, is that it's taking a long time to bring Rickard into line. We've only been toying with him.'

'Until now. We're not toying any longer.'

'Witness old Sharman's death,' Alec Wenner said with an explosive laugh, through a cloud of smoke from a cigarette he had just lit.

His father flinched. But only from the smoke.

Sharon Pratt did not spend money on evening papers, otherwise she might have read of Eva Sharman's death the previous day. As it was, she saw it in the same newspaper that Frank Wenner showed his son; but about an hour earlier.

She immediately determined not to go to work that day. She would call her friend in the typing pool and ask her to tell the superintendent that she was sick. The occasional day of sick leave in the government service was almost an entitlement.

The idea of visiting Mrs Rickard had been in her mind for several days. She felt that if she could only enlist the support of the wife of Steve's employer, she would have achieved something positive.

As matters stood, she was filled with frustration at her inability to mount a crusade. On the single prison visit she had so far been permitted to make, she had promised Steve through held-back tears that she was thinking day and night of ways in which to help him. He had done his best to be stoical while she was there, but seeing him in those conditions had left her feeling like a piece of pulp.

She must do something. She would do something. At first she had decided to phone the social worker who had called on her the day after Steve's trial had concluded. She discovered, however, that she had lost the piece of paper with the girl's telephone number. She remembered that her name was Clare Reynolds, but when she came to look in the telephone directory she found columns of Reynoldses and realised that it was a hopeless quest.

It was then that she decided she ought to make a bolder move and the idea of approaching Miles Rickard's wife entered her head.

And now the announcement of Eva Sharman's sudden and mysterious death gave her the impetus to take such a step.

Accordingly at about half past ten that morning, she found herself on the doorstep of the Rickards' house, 'Grampians', waiting for someone to answer the bell.

Luckily she did not have to wait long for she could feel her resolution beginning to falter as she shifted nervously from one foot to the other.

The young man who opened the door looked her up and down in an appraising fashion and then smiled. Sharon wasn't sure that she liked his smile. It was a bit too knowing.

'Is Mrs Rickard at home?' she asked.

'Which Mrs Rickard do you want?'

'Mrs Miles Rickard.'

'No, she's out and won't be back till midday.' His smile grew. 'As a matter of fact, she's the only Mrs Rickard who lives here, but there was another girl here the other day enquiring after a Mrs Arthur Rickard and I thought you might also be looking for her. Anyway, is there anything I can do?'

'I really wanted to speak to Mrs Rickard,' Sharon said, glancing about her with a worried air.

'Won't her son do? Anyway, why not give him a try?'

'You? Do you mean you're her son?'

'Terry Upton at your service.'

93

'Upton, did you say?' Sharon said in an increasingly bewildered tone.

'My mother married Miles Rickard second time round,' he replied.

'I don't think you can help,' she said, stung by his obvious enjoyment of her confusion.

'That's not fair, you haven't even given me a chance.' He affected a crestfallen expression.

At this point a tear trickled down Sharon's cheek. She felt her plans were in disarray almost before she had started. She turned her face away and opened her handbag, looking for a handkerchief.

'Come in for a few minutes and I'll give you a cup of coffee.' His tone was gentler and no longer bantering.

'Are you sure I'm not disturbing you?'

He shook his head. 'I'm only waiting for a phone call. In fact, I spend the whole of every day waiting for a phone call. From my agent. I'm an actor.'

'Oh . . . are you in something at the moment?'

'No, my love, I'm not. That's why I sit at home waiting for a phone call.' He gave her a rueful grin. 'It'll come eventually. But have no fears, I'm not asking you in either to seduce you or, worse, to drown you in a flood of self-pity.' He struck a comical pose. 'Terry Upton is alive and well, and can make an excellent cup of coffee – amongst other clever feats.'

Following him into the house, Sharon wondered whether she might have misjudged him. First impressions were not always fair.

'Let's go into the kitchen and, while I brew away, you can unburden your soul. I am right, aren't I, you *have* come to unburden your soul?' He laughed at her expression of surprise. 'I was written all over your face, my love. Even a resting actor could see that.'

'Perhaps you also know what I've come to unburden myself about?' she said, with an edge to her voice.

'A spot of trouble with my stepfather? If so, you wouldn't be the first, and assuredly not the last. With some it's drink, with others gambling, with others again it's women. And, of course, there are those who go in for all three and a few miscellaneous pleasures besides. Let me quickly say that I'm

94

relatively abstemious in all respects. My mother has a weakness for gambling and my stepfather for girls. But I can see from your expression it's not that.'

'I've never met your stepfather.'

'Then that accounts for it. But unburden yourself and tell me what *does* bring you to our doorstep.'

'I'm Steve Burley's fiancée,' she said flatly.

'Steve Burley? Steve Burley? Oh, the chap who staged a burglary at Rickard's.' He looked at her with sharp interest.

'He never did it.'

'All right, he never did it, but how can I help?'

'Miss Sharman's dead.'

'So I know all too well. My stepfather's in a great state over it. She'd been with the firm over thirty years.'

'Why did she die?' Sharon cried out in a ringing tone.

'I haven't the slightest idea, my love. Surely you haven't come all this way just to ask me that.'

'It was your mother I wanted to talk to,' she said in a defensively dignified tone.

'Well, take it from me that she couldn't help you any more than I can.'

'Miss Sharman's death must be connected with the burglary.'

'So that's your tack! Chief prosecution witness dies mysteriously, therefore boy-friend wrongly imprisoned. Is that it?'

'I knew he'd never done it before Miss Sharman died. Her death simply proves it. Don't you see that, Mr Upton?'

'Terry. Call me Terry. Only the tax inspector calls me Mr Upton and it's a long time since I was of any interest to him. Incidentally, you've never told me your name.'

'Sharon Pratt.'

'Sharon. I've always liked the name, Sharon. All the Sharons I've known have been particularly nice girls and now along comes another nice one.' He gazed at her with head on one side and a small amused smile.

'Why did Miss Sharman say it was Steve when it wasn't?' she said in a stubborn tone.

Terry Upton sighed. 'My love, how on earth should I know?'

'But you accept that she did?' Sharon pounced like a kitten at a ball of wool.

He flung up his hands in mock surrender. 'I only live here, and I wouldn't do that if I could afford not to. I have nothing to do with my stepfather's business and I know nothing of the machinations that go on there.'

'But you'd met Miss Sharman?' Sharon persisted.

'Met her once and spoken to her on the phone quite often. You couldn't get through to my stepfather without first propitiating the dragon at the gate.'

'She must have mentioned the burglary?'

Upton furrowed his brow in an effort of recollection. 'It upset her. It was a nasty experience for an old dear of her age to come face to face with a masked burglar.'

'That's what she told you?'

'It's certainly the impression I gained. Some of it may have come from my stepfather. He was very upset, too.'

'But whoever it was, it couldn't have been Steve.'

'So you keep on saying, my love, but Eva Sharman thought it was and so, after all, did the jury. Why don't you stop banging your head against a wall?'

'I'll never stop till the world realises Steve is innocent.'

'That's a tall order. I'm still not exactly clear why you've come knocking on our door.'

'I thought I could talk to your mother as another woman. She'd understand.'

'Whether or not she'd understand, I don't see what she could be expected to do.'

'She might know things about Miss Sharman.'

'What sort of things?' His tone had taken on a brittle note.

'Things that would show she was wrong about Steve being the burglar.'

'I find it easier to admire your loyalty than your common-sense.'

'What do you mean?' Sharon said, taken aback.

'What do you expect any of us to be able to tell you now that'll change history?'

'I don't understand.'

'If any of us – though heaven knows what my mother and I could ever have said to help – had had any contribution to

96

make, it'd have been made months ago. But we never did; we weren't there when it happened; the police didn't even take statements from us. And nothing's changed.'

'Miss Sharman's dead. That's changed things,' Sharon said stubbornly.

'So you apparently believe, my love.'

'Surely *your* commonsense tells you that her mysterious death is connected with what's happened.'

Upton's self-amused expression became suddenly mean. 'I think you should realise, Sharon, my love, that some people's patience is not inexhaustible,' he said in a grating tone. 'Eva Sharman's death is not a major event in my life and not even you are going to make it so. If the old dear swallowed a dose of something, that's too bad for her, and I'm ready to leave it to my stepfather to be the grief-stricken member of the family. And you won't find that my mother feels any different from me. So, from that point of view, my love, I fear you've had a wasted journey. There's nothing I can do to help lever your Steve out of prison.' He was the first to break the silence which ensued. 'Why are you looking at me in that strange way?' His tone was sharp.

'I'm sorry, I didn't know I was.'

'Well, you were and it was creepy. I don't like being stared at.'

'I thought actors were used to it.'

'There are stares *and* stares.'

'I'm sorry.'

'Apology accepted.' He picked up her empty coffee mug and took it across to the sink, as though to bring her visit to an end.

Sharon watched him thoughtfully. Then she said, 'Did Mr Rickard ever talk about Steve?'

Although his back was turned on her, she could feel, rather than observe, his annoyance. His shoulders assumed a sudden implacable look.

'I'd never heard his name until he was arrested. Until my stepfather came home and told us what had happened.'

'Mr Rickard found it difficult to accept that Steve could have done such a thing, didn't he?'

'Yes, and told the police so. But if it comes to that, every time you look at a paper, you read of even less likely people than your Steve being nabbed by the police. I've never met your boy-friend, but, if I had, I doubt whether I'd have judged him incapable of a spot of burglary.'

'Well, where's he supposed to have hidden all the money, then?'

'What an extraordinary young woman you are!' he said in a patronising tone.

'If you believe he did it, why haven't they found the money?' Sharon shouted at him.

'Presumably because he hid it too well. There! You asked for that, my love. Now perhaps you'll realise that your journey's wasted.'

Sharon was determined to conceal her dismay from this young man whom, she now decided, she had not misjudged. He was heartless and self-satisfied and she hoped she might one day be given the opportunity of switching off her television if his face ever appeared on the screen.

There was nothing to be gained by prolonging her visit, nor was there now anything to be hoped for in talking to his mother. She had drawn a blank, but perhaps she had expected too much in the first place. All she had done was to provide Terry Upton with a butt for his bantering remarks, and helped him pass part of the morning.

It might have heartened her if she had known that he felt in anything but a bantering mood as he watched her depart.

CHAPTER SEVENTEEN

At about the same time as Sharon was foxing and fencing with Terry Upton in the kitchen of the Rickard home, Detective Chief Superintendent Rudgwick was presiding over a meeting in his office attended by Nick and Detective Sergeant Tarry and Detective Chief Inspector Tatham, who was Tom Tarry's immediate superior in the Serious Crimes Squad.

Rudgwick gave the appearance of chewing a throat pastille as he sat with his forearms resting on his desk, leaning forward in a non-kneeler's attitude of prayer. In fact, he had nothing at all in his mouth and the chewing was no more than an indication of assembling his thoughts.

'Our trouble is this,' he said. 'Until we've established the cause of death, we're stuck on the starting line. We simply don't know in which direction to charge off.'

'Supposing it is murder, who are your suspects?' Detective Chief Inspector Tatham asked. 'You obviously have some in the frame. Our friends the Wenners for a start.'

'Would the Wenners have murdered Eva Sharman just to intimidate Rickard?'

'The answer to that is, the Wenners would do anything. Anyone who stands in their way is crushed. There's enough evidence of that. Or rather that's the snag, there's too damn little *evidence*. It's all rumour and hearsay and informant's tittle tattle. But even if only half it is to be believed, Frank and Alec Wenner should spend the rest of their lives locked up.' Tatham paused and frowned at the lighted tip of his cigarette. 'And your Miles Rickard would appear to be doubly vulnerable. An informant of Tom Tarry's has told him that the Wenners plan to use his premises to store a consignment of hard porn which is expected here shortly from the continent. And then we've also heard that Frank Wenner has a spite to work off against Rickard for the way he treated his daughter. And I wouldn't want to be in the shoes of anyone toward whom Frank felt spiteful.'

'This is what Rickard himself has now told Sergeant Attwell,' Rudgwick said.

'I know. So we have it two ways,' Sergeant Tarry remarked.

Nick now spoke. 'It still seems to me to be a pretty drastic thing to do, even for the Wenners, to kill an innocent old lady in order to bring pressure on a third person.'

'It wouldn't bother them, Nick,' Tarry said. 'Not one little bit would it bother them if it achieved their purpose.'

'Then you don't regard the Wenners as suspects. That is if she *was* murdered?' Tatham asked.

'On the contrary, sir, I'd regard them very much as suspects, but I believe they may have had a stronger motive. I think there may have been some connection between Eva Sharman, the burglary and the Wenners. I think that somehow the Wenners manipulated Eva Sharman. I don't know how or even whether she was a witting or unwitting party, but I feel there could be a link there.'

'As you know,' Rudgwick said drily, 'Sergeant Attwell has come to believe that Burley was wrongly convicted. In fact, that he was framed. Luckily, he has an appeal pending so we're not called upon at the moment to do more than keep our eyes and ears open, though I've no doubt that Eva Sharman's death will be added to the grounds of appeal.' A slow smile broke over his face. 'If Nick Attwell proves to be right, I'm happy to say that I shall have retired by the time the shit starts to fly. As fly it most certainly will.' His jaws began their rhythmic chewing again. 'Apart from the Wenners, we shall want to see where Rickard himself stands if it becomes a murder enquiry. She'd been his secretary for the past five or six years and his father's before that, so heaven knows what dynamite she mayn't have acquired. Most secretaries know enough about their bosses to blow them out of their chairs and the Eva Sharmans with their all-seeing eyes and their ears like radar scanners can become deadly threats overnight.'

'Did this Sharman woman have any family?' Tatham enquired.

'A cousin in Birmingham whom she used to see about once a year. Otherwise no one. The cousin's husband identified the body at the mortuary, but only after a long haggle as to who'd

100

pay his train fare. And when he did arrive, his main interest was in her will.'

'Did she leave one?'

'We found one in a drawer last night. She left her cousin fifty pounds, but otherwise everything went to the R.S.P.C.A. on condition that they find a good home for her cat. At least that's one problem which doesn't belong to us. We've discharged our humanitarian duty by getting a neighbour to look after the animal for the time being.'

Detective Chief Inspector Tatham leaned forward, clasping his hands across his knees.

'I can see that you're stuck until you know the cause of death and I doubt if there's anything further we can usefully discuss. Our position is that, if you do haul in either of the Wenners for questioning, we'd like to have advance notice and arrange for one of our lot to be present.'

Rudgwick nodded. 'Can't object to that.'

After Tatham and Tarry had departed, he turned to Nick and said, 'Serious Crimes Squad, Vice Squad, Drugs Squad, if you ask me we'd be better off if they were all disbanded and the officers transferred to division to help us blokes in the field. Trouble today is that the answer to every C.I.D. problem seems to be to create a new section and give it some fancy label and then fill it with officers who could be better employed elsewhere.'

Nick was saved having to respond by Rudgwick's telephone ringing. This was just as well as his own view was that his Detective Chief Superintendent was a tough and slightly embittered officer whose age and temperament and service had combined to harden his arteries.

He watched Rudgwick's expression change from one of weary disillusionment to wide-eyed astonishment.

'Blimey,' he exclaimed at one point with old fashioned vigour.

When he replaced the receiver, he was still looking startled in a way Nick had never seen before.

'That was one of the lab liaison officers,' he said. 'Preliminary analysis of the dregs in Eva Sharman's bedside cup indicate enough L.S.D. to have sent her on a trip to Mars and back.'

CHAPTER EIGHTEEN

It took Nick over half an hour to trace Professor Travers and it was a further forty minutes before he and Rudgwick ran him to ground in a South London mortuary.

'Caught me just in time,' the pathologist said, peeling off his rubber apron and walking over to the wash basin. 'I have another p.m. in half an hour and we have to get to Southwark.'

'That won't take you long,' Rudgwick said firmly.

'It mayn't the way you people drive,' Travers remarked with a glint in his eye. 'Anyway, what brought you?'

Rudgwick told him and the pathologist let out a low soft whistle.

'Well, well! Not that it comes entirely as a surprise.'

'You mean you'd guessed?'

Professor Travers gave Rudgwick a glare.

'Certainly not! I don't guess in my work. I'd begun to make deductions, which is a very different matter from guessing. I spent a couple of hours with my text books when I got home last night and L.S.D. was one of the possibilities I'd considered.'

'Wouldn't you have expected to have found traces in her body?' Rudgwick asked.

'It's precisely because I didn't find traces of anything that I wondered about L.S.D. It's odourless, tasteless and colourless; moreover, it causes no organic trauma, though a particularly large dose can result in brain damage.'

'Ah!'

'Exactly, ah! You recall that I detected oedema of the brain?' Rudgwick and Nick both nodded. 'What was the quantity revealed in the dregs at the bottom of the cup?'

'They can't say yet. What I got from the lab was by way of a news flash.'

'The normal dosage is around 250 micrograms and that's sufficient to induce a trip lasting up to eight hours. You get some idea of the potency of the drug if I tell you that one microgram is equal to one-millionth of a gram.'

'I already knew that,' Rudgwick said, grimly.

'So now you know it even better. And here's another statistic to rub the point home. It's been estimated that one pound of L.S.D. dropped into the unprotected water supply of a city the size of London would be sufficient to induce a mass psychosis of the entire population.' Professor Travers' eyes danced with the light of challenge. It was almost as if he were about to co-opt them in some mad scientist's scheme.

'All the cases I've heard about,' Nick said, 'have involved the user jumping out of a window thinking he could fly or hurling himself under a bus in the belief that he was indestructible. Why didn't Eva Sharman do something like that?'

Professor Travers nodded keenly. 'A good question. At this stage I can only surmise that the dosage was so large that it induced heart failure before she could go on the sort of trip you mention. On the other hand, the disorder in her room is now explained by the fact that she had obviously become hallucinated in the moments before her death.'

'I've never heard of anyone dying of L.S.D.,' Rudgwick observed.

'And I haven't yet come across a recorded case either,' Travers said with the enthusiasm of a pioneer. 'People have died as a result of jumping out of windows while under the influence of the drug, but the cause of death has always been other than the actual ingestion of L.S.D.' He glanced from one to another of his audience, his appointment at Southwark mortuary temporarily forgotten. 'Another feature of the drug is that the effects can recur. There was a case in the North of England where a man jumped off the roof of a building three days after taking L.S.D. He landed on the roof of a passing car, killing the driver. He himself survived and later stood trial for manslaughter, I understand.'

'It's some sort of acid, isn't it?' Rudgwick asked moodily.

'L.S.D. twenty-five is Lysergamide which is a derivative of lysergic acid which is an alkaloid present in ergot of rye. It's a fungus in the rye.'

103

'You mean that L.S.D. and whisky come from the same source?' Rudgwick said in disgust.

'You're quite safe, Chief Superintendent, diseased rye is required for one and only the best rye for your whisky.'

'Not my whisky. I can't afford to drink the stuff.'

'One of the troubles with the muck – L.S.D. not whisky – is that it's become relatively easy to synthesise. Anyone with some knowledge of chemistry and the basic laboratory equipment could probably manufacture it. That, of course, makes control all the more difficult.'

Rudgwick looked thoughtful. After a pause he said, 'I think we can safely assume that Miss Sharman didn't go on a voluntary trip. That means her bedtime drink was doctored. And doctored with only one intent in mind. To kill her.'

'Can't be any doubt about that,' Travers observed.

'It seems clear,' Nick broke in, 'that someone put the stuff into the bottle of milk which was left on her doorstep. That would fit, wouldn't it, sir?' he asked, looking at the pathologist, who nodded.

'What form was it likely to have been in?' Rudgwick asked.

'Liquid or powder. It might have been either. Even tablet form, with tablets no larger than micro-dots.'

'And it wouldn't have coloured the milk or given it any taste or smell?'

'None at all. Quite undetectable to the normal senses.'

Rudgwick suddenly swung round on Nick with a look of alarm.

'What happened to that half bottle of milk I noticed in the fridge?'

'It went to the lab with various other items of food.'

'Thank heavens! I envisaged one of the neighbours pouring it over her child's cereal.'

'I reckon the cat was lucky not to have been given a saucerful.'

'Damn the cat! We'd better tell the lab to concentrate their attention on that bottle of milk.'

'I've already done that, sir,' Nick said. 'Just before we left, when I was phoning round trying to trace Professor Travers.'

If Nick had expected to be given a pat on the back for his foresight, he would have been disappointed. Rudgwick was not one for handing out praise to his junior officers. As long as he treated them justly he considered they had their due.

Professor Travers walked across to where his jacket was hanging on a peg and put it on.

'As soon as I've finished at Southwark, I'll get back to work on your body. Now we know what induced her heart failure, we can work backwards.' He shook his head slowly. 'It must be one of the most potent drugs known to man. And one of the most puzzling to a pathologist as it's so rapidly assimilated into the bloodstream and leaves no signs detectable by clinical tests.' He glanced up from the floor on which his gaze had been focussed. 'But I'd have got there, even without the shortcut you've given me. Scientific deduction and long experience would have given me the answer in the end, Mr Rudgwick. Scientific deduction, not guesswork, as you suggested.'

They watched him go out to his waiting car, a ten-year-old Rolls-Royce, with a uniformed chauffeur at the wheel. Because of a mildly grotesque appearance, it was fabled that the chauffeur, who had been in Professor Travers' service for twenty years or more, had been fashioned in the laboratory out of spare pieces.

'He may be a damned good pathologist,' Rudgwick growled, 'but he's not also the Commissioner of Police, the Archbishop of Canterbury and the Lord Chief Justice all rolled into one as he tries to make out at times. I know we're just poor bloody detectives who are only fit to interview milkmen. And that's exactly what we're going to do now, find the man who left a pint on Miss Sharman's doorstep the day before yesterday.'

CHAPTER NINETEEN

It did not take long to discover the name of the dairy which delivered milk to Eva Sharman and even less time to learn that Fred Chaytor was the roundsman. They found him with his electric float in a neighbouring street.

'We want to talk to you, Fred,' Rudgwick said from their car which was parked on the opposite side of the road to where the float was temporarily halted.

Fred Chaytor came across and Rudgwick introduced himself. 'Can't leave it,' he said nodding at his vehicle. 'Kids'll nick things or even try and get it going.'

'That's all right, just come and talk in the car and you can keep an eye on it.'

'Not going to take long, is it? I'm behind as it is.'

'Five minutes should be enough. We'll get Sergeant Attwell to sit in front and you get in beside me.' When Fred Chaytor was seated in the car, Rudgwick went on, 'You know Miss Sharman's dead?'

'Took some sleeping pills, didn't she?'

'Could be. Did you deliver her milk the day before yesterday?'

'Yes and yesterday. There was a man and girl trying to get into the house when I called yesterday.'

Rudgwick nodded. 'We know about them. But you're certain it was you who made the delivery the previous day?'

'Of course, I'm certain. I'm on six days this week.'

'Where would the bottle of milk have come from?'

'From my float over there. From one of the crates of silver top. She always had silver top. Didn't like gold top, said it was too creamy.'

'And you collect the crates of milk from the depot?'

'That's right.'

'I take it that nobody could know in advance which bottle you were going to leave on Miss Sharman's doorstep?'

'How could they? Don't know myself. I just lifts one out of the crate when I gets to her place.'

'I understand that Miss Sharman kept a plastic cup on the step for you to put over the top of her bottle?'

' 'Sright. Otherwise the birds would peck away the silver foil.'

'And did you place the plastic cup on top of the bottle the day before yesterday?'

'Yes,' Chaytor said, with a vigorous nod.

'There's no doubt about that?'

'I did it the same like I always did it. Sometimes a relief man who didn't know wouldn't do it and then she didn't half moan. Mind you, I sympathised with her. Anything can get into your milk once the seal's been broken. You don't want to get home and find an earwig or a trail of ants in your milk.' He paused abruptly and gave Rudgwick a suspicious look. 'Are you meaning that something got into her milk?'

'It seems very possible.'

'Well, it could only have been after I'd left it. There was nothing wrong with it before.'

'That's what I'd assume,' Rudgwick said in a mollifying tone. 'What time did you deliver at Miss Sharman's the day before yesterday?'

'It'd've been around ten. That's my usual time for Brocken Road.'

'That means her milk would have stood on the doorstep for about eight hours,' Nick observed.

'Mmm! Well, thanks, Fred,' Rudgwick said, 'we needn't hold you up any longer. We'll want to take a statement from you sometime. Can you come round to the station this evening, say six o'clock?'

'How do I get there?'

'I'll send a car for you. Take you home afterwards as well.'

'Got a darts match at my local at eight.'

'O.K., we can drop you off there.'

Fred Chaytor nodded with pleasure. That would impress his team-mates, might even put off the opposition, he reckoned, as his mind envisaged sirens, flashing blue lights and an escort of motor cycles.

Rudgwick watched him walk across the road to his milk

float, a new spring in his step. 'O.K., Harry,' he said to his driver, 'back to the station.'

Fred raised his hand in casual salute as their car pulled away.

On arrival at the station, Rudgwick disappeared into his office to make a number of phone calls, leaving Nick to organise house to house visits in Brocken Road to ascertain whether anyone had noticed a stranger in the vicinity of Miss Sharman's flat between ten o'clock in the morning and half past six in the evening two days previously.

'You'd better call at every house,' Nick said to the four young constables whom he had been able to muster for the job, 'though obviously it's the people living opposite and in the houses either side you want to concentrate on. Ask particularly whether they saw anyone in official guise, postman, gas board or electricity people. They're apt to be taken as part of the natural scenery and not be mentioned unless you ask.'

'If you want my opinion, sarge,' said Constable Boyd, 'we're likely to get too much rather than too little information. I know that sort of road, probably got more prying eyes than Hampstead Heath on a summer's evening.'

'Let's hope so.'

'Except that a lot of them will have imagined things by now.'

'That's where checking and cross-checking will come in. We should be able to eliminate quite quickly the more improbable sightings. Anyway, get going now and see what you can find out in the next couple of hours.'

Nick returned to his own room which he shared with two other detective sergeants. One of them was on a course at the Hendon Training School and the other had gone off to Sweden to escort back a man who was finally being extradited after a long drawn out battle in and out of the Swedish courts.

Their desks, like Nick's, appeared to have become a dumping-ground for paper. And, worse still, paper requiring some sort of action or other. He knew what action he would like to take with much of it and his waste-paper basket was invitingly empty, but he was never seriously tempted though he knew of one colleague who had managed to 'lose' an enormous dog-eared file which had hung around his neck for months, heavier than any millstone. Indeed, it had sunk immediately when dropped over the parapet of a bridge into the river one dark night. And with its disappearance had withered the pertinacity of the slightly unhinged complainant who was the source of its contents. You obviously had to choose your moment and your file before you could take such drastic action and also be blessed with a certain insouciance of temperament.

Nick looked at his desk and sighed. He had no fewer than thirty-five dockets in various stages of completion, all of them requiring further work when he could get round to it. The public was always apt to imagine, in so far as it gave the matter any thought at all, that an officer gave his undivided attention to one case at a time and only moved on to the next when the previous one was neatly tied up with a bow of ribbon.

Little did the public realise how a detective sergeant on division operated; how he tried to keep as many balls as possible in the air at one time; how his priorities would change from day to day under the pressure of events; and how he would literally drop his pen in the middle of writing a report on a case of housebreaking to go and investigate one of rape. It was like those chess masters who take on a dozen opponents at the same time. Like that, except that it was a good deal less calm.

The phone on Nick's desk rang and he reached for the receiver. It was Rudgwick requiring his attendance.

'I've been through to the fingerprint people,' he said as Nick entered. 'The only identifiable prints in the flat are Eva Sharman's. They found some smudged ones on the back of a chair, which didn't tally with hers, but which weren't clear enough to identify in any event.' He gave Nick a sardonic look. 'Probably your wife's!' Nick smiled in a tentative fashion. 'I've told them to get hold of the milk bottle from the lab and test it. We must remember to take Fred Chaytor's prints when he comes this evening.'

'I'd think that whoever introduced the L.S.D. wore gloves, sir,' Nick said.

'So would I. Murderers make mistakes, but not that sort.' Rudgwick went on, 'I've also talked to the lab. They now reckon that approximately five thousand micrograms of the stuff was put into the bottle. That would be at least twenty times the amount required to send you on a normal trip. If *normal* is the right word.'

'Is that based on an analysis of the contents of the bottle as well as of the dregs?' Nick asked.

'I gather so. They're still busy testing.' He shook his head in a ruminative way. 'It's a wonder the old girl didn't take off through the ceiling. Its the most fiendish thing I've ever come across, and nobody's ever heard me say that before.'

'I wish there were previous recorded cases of death from L.S.D.,' Nick said in a worried voice. 'You know what the defence can do when all the experts are roaming around virgin territory.'

'If a jury doesn't infer an intent to kill in someone who puts that amount of L.S.D. into an innocent bottle of milk, then we can all pack up and put straw in our hair. What else would he have done it for? As a joke? To give her a trip for fun?' He threw Nick a baleful look. 'I've told Detective Inspector Cresson to find out if anyone connected with the case has a history of using drugs. Any drugs. If you can get hold of one, you can get hold of others.' He glanced at his watch. 'I suppose I'd better let the D.A.C. know the score. Otherwise there'll be something in the press and hell on high will break loose because the Yard was taken by surprise.'

When Nick got back to his office, he found an additional piece of paper on his desk. It was a message from the Assistant Governor of Wormwood Scrubs Prison saying that 14203 Burley S. wanted to see Detective Sergeant Attwell urgently in connection with the death of Miss Eva Sharman.

Nick could not imagine that Steve Burley had anything useful to contribute to the enquiry, but realised that he would nevertheless have to go sometime. But it could wait. He suddenly discovered that his feelings toward Burley had become a trifle ambivalent. It wasn't so much that his belief in the young clerk's innocence had diminished as that the focus had changed. He reminded himself of what Clare had said about distances being deceptive. That was true. There wasn't necessarily more than a single step between the burglary and Eva

Sharman's death. If they were connected, it would prove to be an extremely close connection. Of that he was sure.

He decided to drive out to Brocken Road and see how his team of four were getting on with their house to house enquiries. They gathered round his car as soon as they spotted him, their work all but completed.

It was as he had anticipated. Some people had noticed nothing, others with livelier imaginations had made Brocken Road sound like a parade ground of sinister characters on the day in question.

There had been a bearded Indian peddling brooms, a yellow van with nothing painted on its sides parked for over an hour three doors away from Miss Sharman's house while its driver remained motionless within, and a young man with long hair who walked slowly up and down the road staring at people's front doors.

When Nick had listened to all they had to tell him, he said, 'We'll get a loud-hailer van out asking for anyone who was in the neighbourhood of the deceased's house to come forward. We'll also get the press to co-operate. That way we may be able to eliminate most of this lot. The main point is that you haven't found anyone who actually saw a person enter or leave Eva Sharman's premises.'

'It'd be getting dark by the time she arrived home, sarge, so whoever it was may have acted under cover of darkness.'

'I realise that. But it would have to have been within the last half hour. It was an overcast day and sunset was at ten past six.'

'That's when I'd have chosen to do it,' Constable Boyd said, as though this placed the matter beyond argument.

Leaving them to complete their calls, Nick returned to the station, where he immediately phoned Wendy Smith. With luck, she might have a bit of information for him.

She sounded cautious on the telephone, as was to be expected. She said they were all still stunned by what had happened and that Miles Rickard himself wore a positively haunted expression. Otherwise, she had nothing to report, but promised to get in touch with Nick should she see or hear anything of significance.

It was late again when Nick got home that evening and he

111

found Clare putting the finishing touches to Simon's room.

'As soon as the smell of paint has disappeared, I'll go and fetch him home,' she said. 'It doesn't look as though you're going to call further on my services in view of latest developments.'

'You never know,' Nick remarked. 'But it'll be nice to have Simon back, anyway. Peggy next door will always mind him for an hour or two if you have to go out.'

Over their supper, Nick related the day's events. Clare winced when he told her the amount of L.S.D. found in the bottle of milk. She had had a fair amount to do with young drug addicts as a serving police officer and had never become hardened to the appalling effect drugs could wreak on their self-chosen victims.

'It must have been like setting off a charge of dynamite in her brain,' she said.

'I hope it acted as swiftly,' Nick replied.

'So what now?'

'We'd like to find something a bit stronger against them before tackling the Wenners, but I think we'll have to have a go at them anyway.'

'You're not likely to break them unless you do have some concrete evidence.'

'We're not likely to break them. Period.'

'I can see the case developing into a slanging match between the Wenners and Rickard, each side suggesting that the other had motive and opportunity to murder poor old Eva Sharman.'

'The police can be the only beneficiaries of a slanging match,' Nick observed.

'Have the Wenners been involved with drugs, Nick?'

'I don't think so, but they obviously move in circles where procurement wouldn't be a problem.'

Clare watched Nick as he set about his second helping of steak and kidney pie.

'When are you going to see Steve Burley?' she asked in a thoughtful tone.

'Tomorrow; the next day. It depends on the guvnor.'

'I wonder if I could get in to see him?'

Nick gave her a startled look. 'Why on earth do you want to see him?'

112

'To satisfy my curiosity.'

'For God's sake, don't go knocking on the prison gate pretending you're the Home Secretary's wife or anything like that.'

Clare laughed. 'Of course not. If I can't get in legitimately, I shan't get in at all. Don't worry, Nick, I'll not risk embarassing you.'

'Embarrassment will be the least of my troubles,' he said anxiously. 'But seriously, how can you visit him?'

'I mayn't be able to, but I'll have a good think.'

Nick realised from her tone that about the only course open to him was to have a third helping of steak and kidney pie.

CHAPTER TWENTY

It was a few minutes before nine the next morning when two police cars came to a lurching halt in the drive of the Wenners' house and five officers jumped out. Among them were Rudgwick, Nick and Tom Tarry.

While one of them ran forward and gave the doorbell a series of vigorous prods, Rudgwick stood back and surveyed the front of the house.

'Worth about £120,000 at today's prices,' he murmured.

'Don't expect it even has a mortgage,' Nick said. 'Probably paid for in bundles of used notes.'

The door was opened by Helen Wenner who ran a cool eye over the cluster of waiting men. Rudgwick stepped forward.

'Mrs Rickard is it?' he asked.

'My name is now Wenner. Who do you want to see?'

'Are your father and brother at home?'

'I'll go and find out.'

'Don't you want to know who we are?'

'You're police. That's obvious. Just wait here.'

She moved to close the door, but Nick stepped forward and thwarted her intention.

'Don't worry,' he said with a small grin, 'we won't allow any intruders in.'

The decision to go in force had not been taken out of any fear of violence but to impress Frank and Alec Wenner with the serious purpose of the visit.

Frank Wenner now appeared in the hall, walking slowly towards the front door. It was not a slowness resulting from sixty-three years of age, but his own calculated response to their heavy-handed arrival. He didn't run and jump for any police officer was the message conveyed by his approach. He was wearing a pair of perfectly creased fawn slacks and a cream silk shirt unbuttoned at the neck. On his feet were a pair of highly polished crocodile-skin slippers. A faint aroma of after-shave lotion came off him and added to the overall impression of compact well-being. Nick noticed, in particular, the shiny tan leather belt with its gleaming gold buckle which encompassed a waist any male model would have been proud to display.

Rudgwick stepped through into the hall before Wenner reached them.

Just like two old actors, each determined not to be up-staged by the other, Nick reflected.

'I'm Detective Chief Superintendent Rudgwick and these are . . .' Rudgwick introduced each of them by rank and name. 'We'd like to talk to you and your son. Any objection if we come in?' As he spoke he took a further step into the house.

Wenner gave a slight shrug as if to indicate that only good manners prevented his hustling them out and slamming the front door. Turning, he opened a door on the left of the hall and walked through. They all followed to find themselves in a formally furnished drawing-room which, from appearance and smell, was seldom used. It contained a number of arm-chairs and two huge settees, all covered in silver satin adorned with pink roses.

'All right to sit on one of these?' Rudgwick enquired in a sardonic tone, eyeing a chair. He sat down. 'Mind if we smoke?' he asked, and lighted a cigarette before Wenner res-ponded. 'Where's Alec? It'll save trouble all round if he's here from the outset.'

'He'll come when he's finished his breakfast,' his father said, speaking for the first time. He had seated himself on an up-right chair in a corner of the room from where he could watch everyone without having to turn.

At that moment, the door burst open and Alec Wenner entered. He had a large cigar in his mouth and was in every way a bigger and younger edition of his father. It was doubt-ful whether he would ever have his figure, but he radiated strength from every bulge of his muscular frame.

'Quite a party, i'n't it?' he observed looking from face to face. 'Not kept you waiting, I hope.' He walked over to a chair and perched himself casually on its arm. 'Well, what's brought all you gents here on a dawn visit? Can't be you knew it was my birthday.'

115

'It's not,' Sergeant Tarry said. 'I can tell you exactly when your birthday is. I'm less certain, however, where you'll be spending it.'

'Hear that, Frank? Haven't been in the house a couple of minutes and they're starting to threaten us.'

'We want to talk to you about certain things that have recently happened at Rickard's,' Rudgwick broke in.

'Oh, him!' Alec Wenner's voice assumed an air of boredom.

'At least you admit knowing him?'

' 'Course we know him. He was married to my sister for a time.'

'What sort of relationship have you had since their marriage broke up?'

Alec Wenner looked across at his father.

'How'd you describe it, Frank?'

'Haven't had much to do with him,' Frank Wenner said. 'We still have a few shares in the business, but we don't interfere.'

'It's rumoured,' Nick said, 'that you'd do anything to spite Miles Rickard because of the way he treated Helen.'

'There's always a lot of silly talk going round. I thought the police had better things to do than listen to it.'

'But is it true?'

'I don't like Miles Rickard. I never have and, what's more, I've never pretended that I did.' He shrugged. 'So what? I expect there are a few people you don't like.'

'I don't go about threatening them.'

'Who says I've threatened Rickard?'

'*He* does for a start.'

Frank Wenner's stare seemed to harden for a second. 'Rickard's in a mess. He'd say anything.'

'What sort of mess?' Rudgwick asked sharply.

'Every sort of mess, from what I hear.'

'That's right,' Alec Wenner chimed in.

'Tell us, then, what sort of mess he's in?'

'Alec and I don't go in for rumours like some people. Just put your ears to the ground and you'll find out soon enough.'

'So you can't be more specific?'

'I've said my bit about that.' He glanced across at his son. 'And so has Alec.'

116

Rudgwick looked from one to the other. Alec Wenner might be the more talkative, but he clearly took his cues from his father.

'You know that there was a burglary at Rickard's a few months ago?' Rudgwick went on. 'And then a couple of days ago Eva Sharman died suddenly, murdered for sure. We believe you know something about both those events?'

Alec Wenner seemed about to burst out with something, but fell silent on a look from his father.

'What are we supposed to know?'

'Who instigated them. That's what I believe you know.'

'I'm afraid I never had a good education like all you policemen these days. Probably that's why I'm not following you.'

'I'm suggesting, Frank, that you were behind the burglary *and* the murder of Eva Sharman.'

'They must be out of their blue serge minds,' Alec Wenner remarked with an indulgent laugh.

'And what motive am I supposed to have had?' Frank Wenner asked, ignoring his son's comment.

'It could have been a double motive. In part, you were taking your revenge on Rickard, but you were also wanting to intimidate him. He says you were trying to get him to agree to your storing a big consignment of porn on his premises.'

'Rubbish.'

'Don't be too quick to answer. You forget that we can often track a load of porn on its devious route into the country as successfully as the Americans track a space vehicle on its way to Mars.'

Frank Wenner who had abruptly shifted his gaze to the floor slowly raised his eyes to meet Rudgwick's.

'Rickard is talking rubbish. He's lying.'

'Certainly, one of you is,' Nick broke in.

'And it won't take long to discover which,' Rudgwick said. 'You see, it's all one pattern of pressure and intimidation to break Rickard down. By the way, do you know James Tikoritis, or Jimmy the Tick as he's known to his friends?'

'Don't say he's been telling fairy tales about us, too!' Alec Wenner exclaimed.

'Your friends never stop talking about you,' Rudgwick said, baring uneven yellow teeth in an unaccustomed smile. 'I'd

117

thought you'd know him. Let me think now, what's his slogan? "You want it, I can get it." I'm told he can, too. Everything from cannabis to L.S.D.'

'What's he on about?' Alec Wenner said, looking across at his father with an expression of simulated bewilderment.

But once more the older man didn't respond either by word or gesture, and Nick began to wonder whether they might not have been better advised to have seen them separately. It would not have meant getting any more out of Frank Wenner, but Alec's tongue might have wagged better in his father's absence. Not that any of them had expected the visit to produce confessions of guilt. Its main purpose was to warn the Wenners against further intimidation of Rickard, to let them know that they had better watch their step while the police continued to burrow away quietly.

Frank Wenner now spoke, looking round the faces turned toward him like a teacher about to pose a particularly difficult question to his class.

'This burglary at Rickard's you mentioned, how am I supposed to have worked that?'

'Rickard had £20,000 stolen and it's not insured. I'd have thought you found that very sweet.'

'It still doesn't prove I had anything to do with it.'

'You worked it through Eva Sharman and then had to kill her to keep her mouth shut.'

'If you believe that, you'll believe anything.'

'We mayn't yet have got all the details straight, but give us time, Frank, and we shall.'

'You must let me know when you have. I like a good bedtime story.'

Alec Wenner chuckled. 'Me, too.'

'Your luck can't hold for ever, Frank,' Rudgwick went on. 'You've had a long run, but it'll come to an end sooner or later, and my guess is that it'll be sooner. And then your reign as emperor will be over and you'll spend the rest of your days as Her Majesty's guest and there won't be any more heated swimming pools and silk shirts and satin covers on the chairs. But I needn't go on. It may be a long while since you were last inside, but I expect you still remember the routine. Not too good for someone of your age, particularly in the winter and

118

you'll find each winter will be a bit worse than the previous one. That's going to be your lot, Frank, and as for sonny here' – Rudgwick swung round to face Alec Wenner – 'he'll miss his cigars and his women, he may even miss his old dad, but he'll probably get out in ten years or so, a bit flabbier and with as little nous as ever.'

Rudgwick rose to his feet and walked toward the door, pausing only to stub out his cigarette in a virgin clean, green onyx ash-tray. The other four got up to follow him.

'We can find our own way out,' he remarked over his shoulder as he left the room.

'Behaving like the bloody K.G.B.,' Alec Wenner said angrily.

'Forget the K.G.B.,' his father replied curtly. He rose from his chair and sniffed at the air with distaste. 'I never did like the smell of coppers.' He led the way from the room. 'Get Helen to make us some coffee. Black coffee. We've got to talk.'

CHAPTER TWENTY-ONE

Soon after Nick had left the house that morning, Clare put a call through to her half-sister in Sussex. When the receiver was lifted at the other end, she heard sounds that indicated a mixture of glee and strife.

'Hello, Molly, it's Clare. Can you hear me all right?'

'Just about.'

'How's Simon?'

'Boisterous.'

'Can you keep him another day or two?'

'Oh, yes,' Molly replied in a tone which Clare could not help admiring.

'He's not being too troublesome, is he?'

'Oh, no. He seems to be enjoying himself.'

'I'm sure he is.'

'He seems to have got a crush on Emma. He follows her everywhere.'

Emma was Molly's second child and aged seven.

'I hope Emma's flattered.'

'Intermittently.' A distant wail greeted Clare's ears. 'Hang on, I think something's happened,' Molly said euphemistically. It was over a minute before she returned to the telephone. 'It was only Simon and Mark negotiating whose turn it was to have the wheelbarrow.'

Clare could picture the scene. Simon being an only child was reluctant to accept that he couldn't immediately play with whatever his eyes chanced to fall on. Though his cousin Mark was five months older, they were evenly matched in size and determination.

'Mark must come and stay with us soon,' Clare said robustly, feeling that it was the minimum required of her at that moment. 'Simon needs other children around him.'

'When are you and Nick going to do something to remedy that?' Molly enquired. Having a large family herself, she was

120

always interested in other people's efforts in this direction. 'You've always said you wanted three and I don't think one wants to have them too spread out.'

'We're thinking about it,' Clare said vaguely.

'By the way, how is Nick?'

'He's fine. Working very hard, but then police officers always do.'

'Like farmers,' Molly observed, her husband being one. 'Simon's here,' she suddenly broke in, 'would you like to speak to him? Say something to mummy, Simon.'

'Hello, darling, are you being a good boy?' Clare enquired brightly.

'Hello,' came a small, soft and cautious voice, which Clare scarcely recognised for its demureness.

'It's mummy,' Clare heard Molly hiss at the other end.

There followed a short mumble, then Molly said, 'I'd better ring off, Clare. He wants to go to the lavatory. Give my love to Nick and see you in a day or two.'

After replacing the receiver, Clare reached for the telephone directory and looked up the number of Messrs Parton and Co, Solicitors, of London, W.5. She found it and scribbled it down on a piece of paper.

In the immediate aftermath of Steve Burley's trial, she had completely forgotten to mention to Nick that she had recognised the face of the solicitor's clerk who was in Court instructing Mr Chant, the defending counsel.

The clerk's name was George Smythe, an amiable, lazy and, as Clare recalled, somewhat sly young man whom she had met when she was Woman Police Constable Clare Reynolds. Indeed, she had on one occasion covered up for him when he had surreptitiously slipped out of Court one summer's afternoon to go across to the betting shop to find out whether the horse he had backed had won the 3.15. He had been gone scarcely a minute before his presence was required and Clare had, on her own initiative, skipped off to fetch him, being fairly certain where she would find him and had remained straight-faced when he explained to the somewhat peppery barrister his firm was instructing that he had gone out of Court only to fetch a law report he thought counsel might need. Alas, he had not been able to lay his hands on it.

121

Afterwards, in thanking Clare for saving his bacon, he had said that he hoped one day to be able to perform a return service for her.

Well, that day had arrived, Clare decided, as she dialled the solicitors' number.

'May I speak to Mr Smythe, please?' she said when a girl answered.

'I don't know whether he's in yet.'

Clare glanced at her watch. It had not occurred to her that the day had not started for everyone. She seemed to have been up and about for hours. It was a few minutes after half past nine.

She was about to say that she would call back when the girl at the other end said, 'I think he's just coming in now. I'll put you through.'

'Mr Smythe? I wonder if you remember me, Woman Police Constable Clare Reynolds?'

'Good lord, yes. How could I ever forget that cliff-hanging afternoon when Bob's-Your-Uncle won the 3.15 and you rescued me from what could have been a ticklish situation.' He paused. 'I'd have thought you'd have been at least an inspector by now. You deserve to be.'

'I'm no longer in the force. I got married.'

'Well, he's a lucky fellow whoever he is.'

'As a matter of fact, I think you've met him. Detective Sergeant Attwell.'

'Yes, of course I know him. He was the officer in a recent case in which my firm acted.'

'Stephen Burley?'

'That's right! Curiously enough, I'm due to go and see him in the Scrubs this afternoon about his appeal.'

Clare's heart gave a small hopeful leap. 'I'd like to come with you,' she said.

'So that's why you're phoning me?'

'Yes. You said that you hoped one day to return the favour. Here's your chance.'

'I daresay I did, but . . . but this isn't as easy as you appear to believe.'

'Why can't I come as your assistant?'

'You've first got to tell me why you want to come.'

During the next few minutes, Clare explained her interest. She made Nick sound like a neutral spectator as she told George Smythe how she had become persuaded that Burley might be innocent.

'And your husband lets you get up to this sort of lark?' he asked, incredulously. 'And in one of his own cases, too!'

'He's a very fair-minded person.'

'He must be. And why are you so certain that Burley's innocent?'

Clare sidestepped the question and asked one of her own. 'Don't you feel that he may be?'

'He had a good run for his money and the jury convicted him.'

'But he's always protested his innocence.'

'They all do that! Protestations of innocence don't cut much ice when you've been in the defending game as long as I have.'

'What time are you going to see him?'

'Half past three.'

'May I meet you at three o'clock?'

'Where?'

'Any place you suggest.'

'Why do we have to meet half an hour early?'

'So that I can try and persuade you to let me accompany you.'

'Meet me outside the main gate of the prison at three twenty-five,' he said. He was about to ring off when he added, 'I take it this is something entirely between you and me?'

'And my husband.'

'Does he have to know?'

'It may be in Steve Burley's interest that he should.

'It may not.'

'We can discuss it afterwards. You can trust me.'

'The odd thing is that I do.'

So it was that Clare arrived outside the entrance to Wormwood Scrubs at twenty past three that afternoon. She had travelled by public transport and allowed herself time to spare. Five minutes later a taxi drew up and George Smythe got out. He flipped his hand in recognition as he turned his back on her to pay the fare. A few seconds later, he came over to where she was standing.

123

'Hello, Clare. By the way, you don't mind my calling you Clare? But I feel a couple of conspirators like us ought to be on first name terms.' He didn't wait for her to reply, but went on, 'All I want Burley to do is to read through and sign the grounds of appeal. They've been drafted by David Chant. Of course, there may be additional grounds as a result of this visit.' Clare shot him a rapid glance and saw that he was grinning at her in a lopsided fashion. 'Let's go in.'

As they walked across an inner courtyard on their way to the interview room, she said, 'How are you going to explain my presence to Burley?'

'I thought you were to be my assistant.'

'Does that entitle me to ask questions?'

'As many as you want, provided I can listen to the answers. And also provided,' he went on in a more emphatic tone, 'that we discuss afterwards just what is on the record and what is not.'

'That's fair.'

While they were waiting for Steve Burley to arrive, Smythe gazed around the interview room, his nose wrinkled in distaste.

'God, but I feel sorry for the poor sods locked away in these places.' He spoke with a feeling which surprised Clare. 'You might have expected me to be case-hardened by now, but I'm not. At times, I wonder if I perform any more useful function than an attendant at a fairground. I just take the money and set the machinery in motion. The only difference is that my clients don't usually walk out free men at the end of the ride. They're deposited in places like this.' He paused. 'You may well ask why I continue to be a solicitor's clerk if I feel that way. Well, the answer is, because I'm well paid, more or less free to organise my time and too idle to make a change.' He gave her another lopsided grin. 'So you see, I do care, but not enough to do anything about it.'

'I'd have thought that put you in the same category as most of the population.'

It was only at that moment it struck Clare that George Smythe had been indulging in a bit of introspective self-justification when he might have been asking her for details of Eva Sharman's death and of other possibly relevant matters. She recalled that Burley had made disparaging remarks to Nick about his solicitor's clerk and she could understand why. He might be sorry for prisoners in the mass, but it didn't extend to real personal interest in their individual plights.

Burley gave the clerk an unenthusiastic nod when he was brought into the room. His escorting prison officer at once sat down on a chair by the door.

'Hello, Steve, I've brought along your grounds of appeal. They've been drafted by Mr Chant, so I'm sure you'll find them O.K. Just read them through and sign them and we'll get them lodged at the Court.' He noticed Burley starting at Clare. 'This is my assistant, Clare. She's been working on your case.'

Clare gave him a small smile. He had an unhealthy pallor, save for patches of redness caused by shaving, probably, she reflected, with a blunt razor blade and cold water and soap as unforgiving as detergent. The scar beneath his right eye gave the skin a shiny, puckered look.

'Did he say Clare?' he asked, looking at her. Clare nodded. 'Someone called Clare went to see my girl-friend the other day,' he went on, a note of suspicion in his voice.

'It's quite a common name,' she said, trying hard to hide her surge of embarrassment.

'Get on and read those papers, Steve,' Smythe said quickly, pushing the document across the table.

From his expression, as he read, it could have been deduced that he was as unimpressed as his counsel thought the Court of Appeal was likely to be. The main ground of appeal was that the judge had misdirected the jury on burden of proof in general and as to the issue of identity in particular.

'There's no mention of the Sharman woman's death,' Burley said angrily as he reached the end.

'It's hardly a ground of appeal.'

'Of course it is.'

'You tell me.'

'She was chief witness for the prosecution, she lied her head off and now she's dead. Whether it's suicide or murder doesn't matter, it's obvious either way that her death's connected with her lying evidence.'

'I'll tell Mr Chant what you've said. It'll be for him to decide whether to lodge additional grounds.'

Clare decided to put in a word. 'You have to remember, Steve, that the Appeal Court is only concerned with legal argument, it doesn't retry the case.'

'But they can hear further evidence. A bloke in here told me so,' he said, switching his attention to Clare.

'In the first place, the Court itself has to give permission for further evidence to be called and before it does that, it has to be satisfied that the evidence is relevant and for some reason couldn't be called at the Court of trial.'

'Well, of course, it couldn't. She wasn't dead then. How can the judges fail to see that her death proves she was lying?'

'I'll tell Mr Chant everything you've said,' Smythe said wearily. 'It'll be up to him. Now just put your signature at the bottom there.'

Grudgingly, Burley signed the document and pushed it away from him.

'Is it right, I'm not allowed to attend the appeal?'

'Only with the Court's permission. The odds are that it'd be refused in your case. It's not usual for appellants to be present.'

'I suppose that's more of so-called British justice,' he remarked bitterly.

Smythe gave a resigned shrug and looked at Clare as if to indicate the sooner they left, the better he would like it. He clearly had no sympathy with Burley and seemed to regard him simply as a troublesome client with unwarranted demands on his patience and time.

'Has Sergeant Attwell got in touch with you yet?' Burley asked suddenly. 'I told him how Eva Sharman might be Rickard's mother, which would have given her a motive to lie about me.'

Avoiding Smythe's quizzical glance in her direction, Clare said, 'She wasn't ever anyone's mother. She was still a virgin when she died.'

'Good lord!' Burley said with a mixture of surprise and deflation.

'Did you ever hear the name Wenner when you were working at Rickard's?' Clare asked, observing him intently.

'What, a big, tough-looking guy?' he replied with a slight frown.

'That's one of them. There's also his father.'

'I only ever saw one.'

'Ever speak to him?'

'Not that I recall. I didn't see him more than a couple of times or so. He'd be shut away in Mr Rickard's office when he came. What about him, anyway?' he asked in a puzzled tone.

'It was just something I read in your file which made me wonder whether you'd heard his name in the office,' Clare replied vaguely.

'If he's the guy I think he is, I know Eva Sharman didn't take to his visits.'

'How do you know that?'

'You only had to see her face when he was around.'

Twenty minutes later Clare and George Smythe were sitting in a drab little café having a cup of tea.

'I hope you found it a worthwhile visit,' he remarked.

'Yes, I did. I'm very grateful to you for letting me accompany you.'

'What precisely did you learn?'

'That you're going to have a tough time on appeal.'

'Come off it, Clare. You sound as evasive as a politician. What was all that about the Wenners? And, anyway, who are the Wenners?'

'Miles Rickard's first wife was a Helen Wenner.'

'So?'

'They're just part of the landscape and I was interested to know if Burley had heard of them.'

George Smythe gave her an old-fashioned look. Shortly afterwards he paid the bill and they parted company on the pavement outside. As they shook hands he said, 'My firm could use a bright girl like you, why don't you join us?'

Clare's reply was to laugh and give him a wave as she darted for her bus.

When Nick got home that night and told her of the police visit to the Wenners' house, her contribution was to say she was completely satisfied that Steve Burley had never been in tow with either Frank or Alec Wenner. She told him of her own activities that afternoon and how she was sure that Burley had not been simulating when he described the extent of his knowledge of them.

'If you're right about that,' Nick remarked, 'it eliminates another of the possible permutations and helps to confirm our basic premise. Namely that Steve Burley *is* innocent.'

CHAPTER TWENTY-TWO

'There's a Mr Rickard asking for you, sarge,' the constable on duty announced on Nick's extension.

'Tell him I'll be down.'

Miles Rickard was sitting on the edge of a bench fidgeting with a cigarette when Nick arrived downstairs at the receipt of custom. He sprang to his feet as soon as Nick came through the door.

'Any further developments?' he asked anxiously as Nick led the way up to the C.I.D.

He's a bundle of nerves, thought Nick. Aloud he said, 'We just wanted to have a chat with you and felt it'd probably suit all parties better to ask you to come here rather than invade your office.'

Rickard nodded distractedly. 'There are so many rumours going round our place, it'll be a miracle if anyone finds time to sell any cars. I'm sure some of the staff are expecting to see me carted away in handcuffs any moment. I can tell you, Mr Attwell, I'm not finding life much fun at the present time. The sooner you can clear the whole thing up the better.'

They arrived outside Rudgwick's door and Nick knocked. He had already informed his detective chief superintendent of Rickard's arrival.

'Come in and sit down,' Rudgwick said expansively, waving to his visitor's chair. 'There are a number of matters I want to go over with you, but let's start with Miss Sharman's death. She was murdered, Mr Rickard. Poisoned to be more precise.'

Rickard gave the appearance of being hypnotised by Rudgwick's words. Eventually he came out of his trance-like stare and fumbled for his cigarettes. 'I knew she didn't commit suicide,' he murmured, 'she wasn't the type.'

'Someone tampered with the bottle of milk left on her back doorstep,' Rudgwick went on. 'It could have been you.'

Rickard stared at him in horrified disbelief. 'Me?' he said in a croak. 'How could I have done it?'

'Very simply. You left your premises three times that day. Once in the morning, again at lunchtime and once more in the afternoon. Oh, I know you had business appointments, but it wouldn't have taken you more than five minutes to have gone via Miss Sharman's and put poison in her bottle of milk. Shall I tell you something else? Having known her as long as you had, you'd have been aware that birds used to peck off the bottle top if it wasn't covered. Others in your office knew, so you certainly would have done.'

Rickard shook his head as though to rid it of such preposterous suggestions. 'You're not serious?' he said hoarsely.

'I'm entirely serious. Aren't I, Sergeant Attwell?'

Nick nodded. Though he had known that Rudgwick intended roaming over a whole territory of possibilities, he hadn't envisaged a frontal assault on Rickard almost before he had sat down.

Rickard lighted his cigarette and inhaled deeply. It seemed to steady his nerves.

'Eva Sharman was a loyal and faithful employee. I'd known her all my adult life. It's a monstrous slander to suggest I killed her.'

'Was she so loyal that she'd do and say anything to help you?'

'I don't know what you mean.'

'She'd lie for you. Commit perjury even. And then have to be silenced in case the truth came out.'

Rickard had shown increasing agitation as Rudgwick had gone on. 'None of it's true. She never committed perjury. She was always certain it was Burley.' He turned to Nick. 'You never doubted her word, did you, Mr Attwell?'

'I never had any reason to at that time,' Nick said cautiously. 'She certainly struck me as a truthful witness when I interviewed her about the burglary.'

'And the jury and the judge believed her.'

'Yes.'

'So why are you now saying that you and the judge and the jury were all wrong?'

'It's what's happened since.'

130

'Poor Eva gets murdered, so you decide she must have had some guilty secret. I just don't follow you.'

'Why do *you* think she was murdered, Mr Rickard?' Rudgwick broke in.

'I know why she was murdered and I know who did it.'

'Go on,' Rudgwick said, watching him intently.

'She was murdered in order to bring pressure on me.'

'By the Wenners?'

'Yes.'

'A bit of a coincidence isn't it, that she's killed so soon after you'd forecast something of the sort?'

'I know the Wenners.'

'Of course, some nasty-minded person might think you were trying to pin something on the Wenners in advance of the event. It'd be quite a clever trick.'

Rickard looked at Nick with a pleading expression as if to enlist his support against such imputations. 'It's the Wenners you should be third-degreeing. I've told you, haven't I, Mr Attwell, of all the pressure they've put on me? They're in the big-time league, they're ruthless and without pity. Get them put away and you'll be doing everyone a good turn.' He stubbed out his cigarette with a hand that trembled. 'I'd even be prepared to give evidence against them,' he said with a note of emotion. 'I'll help the police in any way I can. There are not many who are prepared to stick their necks out where Frank and Alec Wenner's interests are involved.'

But Rudgwick appeared not to be impressed by Rickard's offer to help. Nor for that matter was Nick, who was thinking that it would be nice to put the Wenners and Rickard in a box together and then shake it until the truth fell out.

'I won't beat about the bush any longer,' Rudgwick said, as if this was the exercise in which he had been indulging until then. 'The Wenners suggest that you're the person who knows more about Eva Sharman's death than anyone else.'

'But you don't believe them?'

Rudgwick shrugged. 'We're still at the stage of asking questions and listening to the answers.'

'But they've no evidence! Whereas there is evidence against them.'

'Only yours.'

'Why shouldn't my word be believed?'

Rudgwick made no reply, but pushed away some papers on his desk in a gesture of impatience.

Nick decided to pursue his own line of thought. 'Don't you think the Wenners could have brought more effective pressure on you and with far less trouble to themselves? I mean, organising that burglary was a far more elaborate scheme than was necessary if all they wanted was to persuade you to let them use your premises for storing porn. Similarly, murdering Eva Sharman seems out of all proportion to their object.'

'Not to the Wenners, Mr Attwell. They'd have arranged the burglary because they knew how much the loss would injure me.'

'How would they have known your office safe happened to be broken and the money was in a desk drawer?'

'Hah! Fifth column. Don't ask me who! I only wish I knew. But it's been apparent for a long time that very little goes on in my office which the Wenners don't learn about almost as soon as it's happened. And as for the murder of poor Eva, they'd know just how deeply it would affect me. In fact, I did crack, but not in the way they intended. I came and told you everything.'

Rudgwick let out a snort. 'As Sergeant Attwell says, it all seems pretty far-fetched.'

'Nothing is too far-fetched when Frank Wenner is out to get his way, particularly if revenge plays a part. He's never forgiven me for marrying his daughter.'

'Or for the way you treated her, from what I hear,' Rudgwick remarked brutally.

Rickard gave him a pinched look. 'There are two sides to every marriage,' he said in a stiff tone.

Rudgwick shifted noisily in his chair. 'Well, is there anything else you want to tell us?'

'Nothing, but I hope you'll give full thought to what I have said.'

'Don't worry, we'll do that all right and we'll be in touch with you again, that's for sure. Show Mr Rickard out, will you, sergeant?'

On his return to his own office, Nick went to the cupboard where he kept most of his case papers and burrowed for the

132

file which bore Stephen Burley's name. He slapped it against his leg to remove an accumulation of dust and carried it over to his desk.

Somewhere within its contents, he felt, lay the clue to everything that had happened.

He turned to Eva Sharman's statement which had provided the beginning and the end of Burley's prosecution.

'Eva Muriel Sharman,' it said at the top and then set out her address. Her occupation was shown as 'secretary' and her age had been tactfully left blank. His eye came down to where the statement proper began.

'I am the secretary of Mr Miles Rickard, the chairman and managing director of Rickard Motor Distributors Limited and have been employed by the company for over thirty years. My office is situated on the corridor above the showroom and is next to Mr Rickard's. I never go out to lunch but take in an apple and a piece of cheese which I eat in my office. I also make a small pot of tea. About the middle of August it was discovered that a fault had developed in the safe in Mr Rickard's office which meant that it couldn't be opened. The manufacturers sent a man to look at it, but he was unable to repair it on his visit and was due to return a few days later. I believe there was some difficulty in getting the necessary spare part. In the meantime Mr Rickard decided to keep cash in a drawer of his desk. So far as I'm aware, only he and I knew of this temporary arrangement. I certainly did not mention it to any other member of the staff. Customers very often pay in cash which means that large sums are on the premises until they can be banked. The usual practice is for money to be taken to the bank at half past two every afternoon. I understand that there had been three or four cash sales during the morning of Thursday, 19th August and that Mr Rickard had put about £20,000 into his desk drawer before going out to lunch. The key to the drawer is missing and so it cannot be locked. I do not know when the key was lost.'

Nick recalled having asked Rickard what had happened to the key and having received a somewhat vague answer that it had disappeared months previously. Knowing that drawer keys had a natural habit of vanishing and their disappearance going unnoticed, Nick had not pursued the point further.

Eva Sharman's statement continued:

'At about one thirty that day, I left my office to go and fill my electric kettle with water to make tea. While I was in the corridor, I thought I heard a faint noise come from Mr Rickard's office. It was a sort of click as of a drawer being closed. The door of his office was shut. I was about to go and investigate when the door opened and I was face to face with someone who had a stocking pulled over his head. I stepped back in alarm and the person seemed to trip slightly as he shot through the door and ran down the stairs which led to the side entrance. He was out of the building before I had recovered from my shock. I then immediately ran down to the showroom and asked someone to phone for the police. I went downstairs because I was the only person in our corridor. All the others were out at lunch. The person who dashed out of Mr Rickard's office was carrying a blue airline bag. I think it had British Airways on it, but I can't be sure. The person had cut eye slits in his mask. One slit, the right one, had torn, slightly enlarging the aperture, and I could clearly see a scar beneath the person's eye. I have no doubt whatsoever that the person was Stephen Burley. Not only did I recognise him from his scar, but I also recognised his jacket. It was the one he always wears to work and has a small black and white check pattern. I did not see Burley again that day. I understand that he came back about half past two. The police had arrived by that time and he was taken away for interview.'

Which was the point where Nick himself had entered the scene. He had taken Eva Sharman's statement that evening and a pretty good statement it was too, he reflected as he read it through, thanks to his judicious guidance. The important thing in taking a statement was to get down the full story without the irrelevances into which witnesses were prone to stray.

And when it had come to giving evidence at the Old Bailey, her oral testimony had scarcely been a comma different from the statement at which he was now looking.

Deep in thought he turned to Rickard's statement.

'Miles Rickard of Grampians, Arcott Avenue, Greenford. Company director. Age 43. I am chairman and managing director of Rickard Motor Distributors Limited. A few days ago the safe in my office became jammed and couldn't be opened. I phoned the manufacturers and a man came to look at it, but was unable to do anything at that stage. He did open it, but it required a spare part before it could be used again as it was impossible to lock. I decided that, in the meantime, it would be best to put cash in the bottom drawer of my desk. It would be out of sight at the back of the drawer and I placed other things on top to hide it. Cash sales are a common feature of our business and that is why we always go to the bank in the afternoon just before it closes so that the only cash on the premises overnight is from sales late in the day. My office desk belonged to my father and the various keys to its drawers have become mislaid and lost over many years. The key to the drawer in which I put the money was the last to disappear. I found it had gone several months ago but didn't regard it as an event of much significance. On Thursday, 19th August, I had placed about £20,000 in the drawer in question just before I went to lunch. I had lunch at home with my stepson. My wife was out. After placing the money at the back of the drawer, I covered it with a folder of correspondence. I also put a similar folder in the front of the drawer, so that anyone opening the drawer would have to move the folders before the cash came to view. It was in ten- and twenty-pound notes. I can't tell you the exact amount in each denomination. I went out to lunch at about 12.45 and came back around two o'clock after I'd been telephoned at home and told about the burglary.

Stephen Burley had been a clerk in our company for about six months. His work has been quite satisfactory. I

135

didn't really know him other than to say "good morning" to. I was shocked to hear that he was the burglar as he had always seemed a quiet and respectable young man.'

When he went home that evening, Nick took the Burley file with him. After he and Clare had finished their supper, he gave it to her.

'Just read Eva Sharman's and Rickard's statements,' he said, 'and tell me what, if anything, strikes you?' She gave him a questioning look and he added, 'There's no trick, it's just that I'm sure we've got to go right back to the beginning in order to solve this crime.'

While she was reading, he prowled about the room, occasionally lifting up ornaments as if they might be concealing clues and then replacing them with studied care.

'Well?' he said when he saw that she had reached the end of the second statement.

'It's all a bit too pat,' she remarked, holding up Rickard's statement. 'The broken safe, the unlockable drawer and a huge sum of money. How would the burglar have known there'd be all that money there on that particular day?'

'I suppose any member of the staff could have found out. After all, I don't suppose the morning's cash sales were a secret.'

'So it was an inside job. It was either Burley which we doubt, or it was deliberately fixed to incriminate Burley. And who'd have fixed it other than Rickard himself?'

'The Wenners.'

Clare made a face. 'That's if one accepts everything that Rickard says, and I don't think I do.'

'If it was Rickard, then Eva Sharman must have been in it, too. Some part of the plan went awry which forced her into making a false accusation against Burley. It would then have been Rickard who did away with her in order to preserve his own skin.'

'It doesn't make sense,' Clare said with a puzzled frown. 'If you're right why did he wait nine weeks before killing her? You'd have expected he'd either have done so immediately after the burglary or not at all. If you're right, something must have happened after the trial which made her a greater danger to him.'

'What?'

'Supposing she had supported him in some false belief and only subsequently discovered the truth?'

'Go on.'

'That would explain the interval of time between the making of his statement and the day of her death.'

'But what was the false belief?'

'I don't know,' Clare said slowly. 'Either it happened just as Eva Sharman testified or she invented it.'

'You mean, she may have invented it without realising the full implication. And when she did, Rickard was forced to kill her.'

'Yes; supposing Rickard got her co-operation by telling her half-truths and by persuading her how important it was she should help him, her subsequent disillusionment when she found out the true nature of events could have made her extremely dangerous to him. Her loyalty wouldn't have stretched to being a willing party to crime, assuming we're arguing from the right premise, namely that she wasn't a deliberate perjurer.'

'The trouble is she can no longer help us find the truth.'

'I'm not sure she'd have been able to even if she'd lived. Any more than Burley can.' She gave Nick a long, thoughtful look. 'I believe there's only one person who can supply the answers and that's Miles Rickard.'

'What about the Wenners? Where do they fit in?'

'I don't know, but my advice would still be not to lift your eye off Rickard. He's the person right at the centre of the web.'

Nick was to recall Clare's words the next afternoon, when he was indeed, finding it difficult to lift his eyes off Rickard. A Miles Rickard lying on a mortuary slab.

CHAPTER TWENTY-THREE

Pamela Rickard always slept with pads over her eyes and plugs in her ears. If she didn't, then even the paperboy on his bicycle was liable to wake her, let alone an early ray of daylight etched round the heavy curtains. Or so she was constantly telling her friends.

When she awoke on this particular morning, she realised that Miles was not beside her in bed. This could only mean that he was shaving in the bathroom and it would soon be time for her to get up. He usually roused her just as he was finishing dressing.

Sleepily she turned over on her other side and drifted deliciously away into a light doze. About twenty minutes later she stirred again. This time she cautiously lifted one eye pad. The bedroom was quite light and she hastily pulled off the other and propped herself up on an elbow. Extracting her ear plugs, she listened intently for the sound of Miles taking his shower, but the whole house was utterly silent. The clock on the small table on his side of the bed showed ten minutes past eight.

For some reason he must have decided not to disturb her. In that case, he would be downstairs getting his breakfast. She sniffed, but could smell neither coffee nor toast. Considerably puzzled, she slipped out of bed and went to the door where she took another deep breath. But there were no breakfast smells and the house seemed more silent than ever. Turning back into the room she noticed that her husband's clothes still lay on the chair where he had placed them the night before; also that his pyjama jacket was not lying at the bottom of the bed where he normally threw it when he was getting dressed. He never wore pyjama trousers.

She put on her dressing-gown and hurried to the bathroom. It was deserted and showed no sign of recent use.

At the top of the stairs, she hesitated. Should she go and wake Terry or go down and investigate on her own? Still reluctant to face the fact that something serious had happened, she decided not to disturb him for the time being.

There were some letters on the mat and the morning paper was half-way through the slit. The curtains were still drawn across the windows in the drawing-room and dining-room, as well as in Miles' small study. She noticed that the cover was off his typewriter, but thought nothing of it.

By now she was in the grip of a mounting fear as she darted into the kitchen. It was exactly as she had left it when she had retired to bed.

She was about to dash upstairs and wake Terry when a faint sound came to her ears. For a second she couldn't identify it and then with a small choked scream she rushed into the small lobby which led off the kitchen and from which there was a door into the garage. Even as she got to it, she knew what to expect. She could see newspaper wedged beneath the door and she had to pull hard in order to open it.

The garage light was on and she could see Miles slumped over the steering wheel of his car. Her eye also took in a length of hosepipe running from the exhaust through the driver's window which was open just enough to admit it.

Choking from the fumes, she reeled back and slammed the door.

'Terry,' she screamed. 'Terry, wake up. Terry, come quickly.'

She was half way up the stairs when he emerged from his bedroom, rubbing his eyes.

'Come quickly, Terry,' she gasped. 'Something awful has happened to Miles.'

Clutching his pyjama trousers with one hand and pushing his hair back with the other, he came running down, his slippers slapping noisily with each step.

'He's in his car. The engine's running. You'll have to open the garage doors in the front otherwise you'll be overcome by the fumes.'

Terry Upton didn't pause to ask questions, but charged out of the front door and round the side of the house to the garage entrance.

'The key, the key,' Pamela Rickard wailed, hurrying after him with the garage key.

He snatched it from her and a second later had pulled open the large double doors. Holding a handkerchief over his mouth and nose, he charged inside and wrenched open the driver's door of the car. As he did so, Miles Rickard's body fell sideways against him and he thrust it back, at the same time reaching for the ignition key and switching off the engine. Then coughing and spluttering he turned and ran back into fresh air.

'There's nothing to be done for him,' he said. 'He's dead. We must phone the police.'

'He might still be alive,' his mother said, making to push past him.

'Don't go in, mother. It'll be some time before the air has cleared. He's definitely dead. You only have to take one look at him to know that. Let's go inside and start telephoning.'

At Pamela Rickard's insistence, he called the ambulance service in addition to the police.

'I'll make some coffee while we're waiting,' he said. 'We both need something.'

His mother, meanwhile, had slumped down on a chair in the breakfast alcove.

'What's that?' she cried out suddenly.

'What's what?'

'That envelope,' she said, staring at a plain unmarked envelope on the table. 'There's something in it.'

Terry Upton came across from the stove and picked it up. It was unsealed and he extracted a folded sheet of paper. It was the paper used by his step-father for typing notes and memos.

His mother watched him in petrified fascination as he read. With a grim expression, he passed the piece of paper to her, but she shook her head.

'You read it to me,' she said in a whisper.

'It just says this: "I'm sorry to do this, but life has become unbearable of late. The last straw has been the police suspecting me not only of arranging to burgle my own premises, but, far worse, of killing poor Eva Sharman. Well, Frank Wenner and his son have given the screw one turn too many and I'll soon be out of their clutches for good. With love to my dearest wife and to my stepson, Terry. I'm sorry that one of you will have the nasty business of finding me. Be careful when you open the garage. Miles." '

Large tears fell down Pamela Rickard's cheeks as she stared at the wall in numbed disbelief. Her son refolded the note and put it back in the envelope. Then he walked over to the stove to fetch the coffee. He had barely poured out two mugs when there was a vigorous ringing of the front-door bell.

'That'll be the police now,' he said.

CHAPTER TWENTY-FOUR

Nick was given the news of Miles Rickard's death as soon as he arrived at the station that morning. It was a few minutes after nine o'clock and he left immediately for the house. He knew that Rudgwick was going direct to a meeting at the Yard and would not be in until the middle of the morning.

By the time he arrived at 'Grampians', most of the activity had died down. Rickard's body had been removed and the various uniformed officers who had attended the scene had departed, save for one young constable who had been told to stay and keep an eye on things. He had interpreted this by stationing himself outside the garage.

Nick caught a glimpse of him as he walked up to the front door and went round the side of the house to speak to him. He was one of the officers who had helped to control by-standers outside Eva Sharman's home on the morning after her death and so knew Nick by sight. It always caused Nick a faint mixture of embarrassment and irritation when he had to introduce himself to a fellow officer at the scene of a crime. He didn't expect every officer in the division to know him by sight, any more than he knew all of them by name, but, for all that, he always felt mildly absurd in declaring himself.

'Good morning,' he said with a smile as he approached.

' 'Morning, sir,' said P.C. Ridd, who, though recognising Nick, couldn't recall his rank and decided to play it safe and drop in a 'sir'.

'You the only officer here?'

'Yes. The others left about fifteen minutes ago.'

'Who's in the house?'

'Just Mrs Rickard and her son.'

Nick nodded and peered inside the garage whose double doors were wide open.

'That's the car he was in,' P.C. Ridd said, indicating a Volvo.

A length of hosepipe ran from its exhaust to beside the driver's door, which was open.

'Show me how it was before he was moved,' Nick said.

The young constable did so and remarked, 'Inspector Parkington says it was a classic case of suicide.'

Nick made no comment. This might well be Inspector Parkington's view, but the uniformed inspector was unaware of all the preceding ramifications. Nick would have liked to have had the garage and car checked for fingerprints, footprints and other possible clues, but he was half an hour too late. Not that he could blame those who had arrived first on the scene. It had appeared a straightforward case of suicide and they had done their job accordingly. Perhaps it *was* a straightforward case of suicide, though, at the moment, Nick was not ready to make any concessions.

Hearing the sound of footsteps, he turned his head to see Terry Upton coming toward the garage. Though he had never met him, he had no difficulty in recognising him from Clare's description.

'Mr Upton? I'm Detective Sergeant Attwell,' he said, stepping forward.

'Ah! I've heard my stepfather mention your name. I saw you walk up the drive and came round to see what was happening.' He was wearing an old pair of grey corduroy trousers, a dark green high neck sweater and a pair of sandals. Taking in these details, Nick noticed that he hadn't shaved that morning.

'Perhaps we can go inside and you'll tell me everything that's happened,' Nick said.

'Yes, surely. My mother's lying down upstairs,' he remarked as they entered the house. 'Shall we go into the kitchen? There's still some coffee left. Or are you hooked on canteen tea?' Noticing Nick's expression, he went on, 'Oh dear, now I've probably shocked you. A mourning stepson oughtn't to make flippant remarks like that, I suppose.'

A death in the family certainly did not seem to have affected Upton's capacity for facetious observations, Nick reflected. No wonder Clare had found him hard to take.

'Tell me exactly what happened?' Nick said, when they

143

were both seated in the dining alcove with mugs of sweet, lukewarm coffee.

When Terry Upton had finished, Nick asked, 'Where's the note your stepfather left?'

'The inspector took it with him.'

'Can I see the typewriter?'

Upton frowned. 'Surely. What do you expect to find on it?'

'I'd just like to see it,' Nick replied.

Taking their coffee with them, Upton led the way across the hall to a small room which faced out the opposite side of the house from the garage. On a desk, set against the window, was a portable typewriter.

'He normally kept it in its case beside his desk when it wasn't in use.'

'I'd like to take it away.'

'Whatever for?' Upton said in a startled tone.

'Various tests.'

'Isn't that unusual?'

'Not as far as I'm concerned,' Nick replied. 'Everyone may be satisfied that your stepfather committed suicide and they may all be right, but too many strange things have been happening in his affairs for other possibilities to be automatically excluded.'

'The first lot of police who came didn't have any doubts.'

'Did they examine the premises thoroughly?'

'Yes.'

'No signs of a forcible entry at any point?'

'None, I gather.'

'Could anyone have got into the garage from outside?'

'Not without a key unless he forced the doors. They're bolted on the inside and there's a Yale lock as well. We normally open them from the inside as they're much easier to push open than to pull from the outside. The wood's swollen and they're apt to stick.'

They both turned as a voice spoke from the doorway. 'Who is it, Terry? I heard voices.'

Pamela Rickard had put on a purple trouser suit and had tidied her hair since her last appearance downstairs.

'This is Detective Sergeant Attwell, mother. He's from the C.I.D.'

144

'I know your name,' she said, giving Nick a limp hand. 'Weren't you the officer who investigated the burglary at my husband's premises?'

'Yes.'

Her mouth trembled. 'Then you're partly responsible for driving my husband to take his life. You've seen the note he left?'

'No, but your son has told me its contents. I assure you, Mrs Rickard, the police have done no more than their duty.'

'I say "partly",' she went on, as though he had not spoken, 'because the people really responsible are Frank Wenner and his family. He's been persecuting my husband for as long as he's known him. He always swore he would see my husband dead and now he's had his way. Only I know what hell and torment my poor Miles suffered at the hands of that crook. He's the person who should go to prison and I hope the police will see that he's put there.'

'I quite understand how you feel,' Nick said quietly. 'If you're up to it, I'd like to have a few words with you about recent events before I go.'

She nodded. 'Yes.' She turned to her son. 'Would you go down to the shops, Terry, I'm out of cigarettes?'

'Are you sure you'll be all right?' he asked, casting Nick a suspicious look.

'I shan't be if I don't have any cigarettes,' she replied.

'Am I allowed in the garage to get the car out?' he asked sulkily. 'My mother's car, not exhibit one.'

'Yes; tell P.C. Ridd I said it'd be all right,' Nick said.

After he had gone off, Pamela Rickard led the way into the drawing-room.

'He hates leaving the telephone at this time of day even for half an hour,' she said vaguely. 'He's always afraid his agent will call and, because he's not in, he'll lose some part which'll then go to Michael York or Peter What's-his-name.'

'Who is his agent?' Miles enquired.

'Len Meyerson in Charing Cross Road,' she said promptly, having obviously been well schooled to provide this important piece of information to any enquirer.

Clare had told Nick that, from a quick peep into the drawing-room as she stood at the front door, it had given the impression of being expensively furnished. Even to Nick's less experienced eye, it clearly was so. The predominant colour was apricot, but with contrasting splashes of other colours in the curtains and wall panels.

Pamela Rickard sat down in a deep armchair and reached for the cigarette box on the glass-top table in front of her. More in hope than expectation, it seemed, she opened it and let out a small satisfied sigh as a single cigarette met her gaze. She seized it greedily and lit it with a silver lighter, held in a hand which trembled. She inhaled deeply and was then ready to give her attention to Nick.

'I'd like to hear your account of the events leading up to the discovery of your husband this morning,' he said.

'Miss Sharman's death had left him very depressed and your interview with him two days ago did nothing to help,' she said in a bitter tone. 'And all the time there were the Wenners pressurising him. He felt that no one understood his difficulties.'

'Did he tell you exactly what they were?' Nick broke in.

'Weren't the Old Bailey trial, Miss Sharman's death and the Wenners constantly on his back enough for anyone?' she asked fiercely. 'Not to mention running a small business in the present economic climate! I didn't have to know any more.'

'Did he talk much about the Wenners?' Nick asked, ignoring her outburst of indignation.

'No, but I could always tell when they'd been worrying him.'

'Did he ever tell you why they were putting pressure on him?'

'It was spite on Frank Wenner's part because of the divorce.' Her voice became shrill as she went on, 'Do you know that Miles was having to pay her alimony even though the Wenners have ten times more money than us? Filthy ill-gotten gains in their case. My poor Miles; in the end he felt that everyone's hand was against him.'

'Did he ever tell you that the Wenners wanted to use his premises?'

'Use his premises? What for?'

'To store some of . . . of their property,' Nick said and went on quickly, 'I'm afraid I've made you digress, Mrs

146

Rickard. Tell me about last night. What time did you go to bed?'

'Miles went up about half past eleven and I followed him about a quarter of an hour later. I waited to see the end of something on television. He was in bed, but still awake when I came up.'

'Had he seemed his normal self during the evening?'

'As I've told you, he'd been worried and depressed for several days.'

'But he wasn't so more than usual last night?'

'No, but these things build up, don't they? They're accumulative.'

'Did he receive any telephone calls during the evening?'

'I don't remember any. I think the phone only rang twice and each time it was for me. Once was my sister in Manchester and the second time it was my friend, Sheila.'

'Was your son at home?'

'No, he usually goes up to the West End in the evenings. I let him take my car.'

'What time did he get back?'

'I heard him tell one of your people, it was about two o'clock.'

'And he then put the car away and locked the garage?'

'Yes and came into the house through the door which leads into the little lobby off the kitchen.'

'Did you hear him come home?'

'No, I never do. He comes up very quietly and, anyway, I always wear ear-plugs at night.'

'Did you have any conversation with your husband when you came up to bed?'

'I told him the end of the programme hadn't been worth sitting up for and that was about all. He just smiled, but in a rather distant way, and went on watching me undress.' In a a slightly brittle tone she went on, 'It seemed he suddenly wanted to make love when I got into bed. I say "suddenly", because it was as if a sudden desire took him.' She gave a small shiver. 'Anyway, we didn't, and soon after that I fell asleep.'

Nick speculated that Pamela Rickard was one of those women who endured rather than enjoyed sexual contact. At all events, one interpretation of her husband's conduct the previous night was that he was seeking one final moment of physical rapture in the knowledge it would be his last.

'After you had gone to sleep, were you aware of his presence at any stage during the night?'

'I always wake up once or twice and turn over and he was still in bed then.'

'Have you any idea what time that would have been?'

'I can only say that it's normally between three and four and then again some time after five.'

'And he was still beside you on each occasion?'

'Definitely. The doctor thought he'd been dead between one and two hours.'

'That would mean he went down to the garage between six and seven o'clock.'

'I suppose so. He must have gone into his study first and typed that note which we found on the table.' She blinked away a tear as she recalled the moment.

'Apart from the problems you've mentioned, did your husband have any other worries of which you're aware?'

'What are you getting at?'

'How did he get on with his family and friends?'

'I don't know what you're suggesting, but ours was an extremely happy marriage,' she said in a tone which bridled. 'We'd both been married before and knew the sort of misunderstandings which can arise. Miles never denied me anything,' she added defiantly.

But I bet you cost him a bit, Nick reflected. Aloud he said, 'How did he get on with your son?'

'They were always good friends. It wasn't easy for Terry living at home with a stepfather, but he used to go out of his way to be nice to Miles.'

No mention, Nick noted, of Rickard's feelings in having an out-of-work stepson squatting in his home.

'I believe your husband's mother is still alive?'

Pamela Rickard sniffed. 'I scarcely know her. We haven't met more than three or four times. She's a bit eccentric.'

'Did your husband see her often?'

'Only when duty required,' she said. 'He was never at all close to his mother.'

148

'Had he ever talked about suicide?'

'Never. But then the ones who talk about it never actually do it.'

'Did he tell you whom he suspected of murdering Miss Sharman?'

'He was so upset by her death, he could hardly bring himself to refer to it. He was genuinely shattered.' Another tear began to roll down her cheek and she dabbed at it with the tissue she clutched in her hand. 'But he was sure it was the Wenners who did it.'

'He told you that?'

'He just said, "It's those fiends" and of course I knew what he meant.'

'Do you have the slightest doubt, Mrs Rickard, that your husband committed suicide?'

'Of course he committed suicide. What else are you suggesting?' she asked in a tone of bewilderment.

'That he might have been murdered?'

'If driving someone to their death is murder, then he was murdered – by Frank Wenner.'

It was a few minutes later while she was showing Nick the upstairs room that Terry Upton returned. He was standing in the hall when they descended.

'You wanted to take my stepfather's typewriter with you,' he said to Nick. 'Here it is. I've put it in its case.' He held it out and Nick took it from him.

Before returning to his own headquarters, Nick decided to call on Inspector Parkington at the local station. On his way, he tried to assess the outcome of his visit to 'Grampians'. Terry Upton had struck him, as he seemed to strike everyone, as a facetious and self-satisfied young man. People were often said to possess surface charm. Well, if Terry Upton possessed any charm at all, it was well-buried charm. As for his mother, Nick found it difficult to know what he thought of her, in particular to decide what had been her true feelings toward her husband. She was doubtless shocked by his death, but did it go deeper than the shock most people experience in the face of sudden death?

He was still pondering the matter when he arrived at Inspector Parkington's station. The inspector was one of those men with a youthful face and a bald head, whose age might have been anything between thirty and forty-five.

Nick told him something of the background and Inspector Parkington let out a soft whistle.

'I only knew some of that. No wonder he'd reached the end of the road.'

'You've no doubt, sir, that it was a genuine suicide?'

'Absolutely none. We obviously made a thorough check of the garage and house and there was no suggestion of foul play. And, of course, there was the note.'

'I'd like to have that, sir,' Nick said.

Inspector Parkington frowned for a moment. 'If I let you have it, you'll have to be responsible to the coroner.'

'That's all right, sir. Incidentally, have arrangements been made for the post mortem?'

'I was speaking to the coroner just before you came. I gather Professor Travers will perform it later today, probably sometime this afternoon. The coroner thought it ought to be the professor as he'd done the p.m. on Mr Rickard's secretary.' He paused. 'I suppose it's occurred to you that the suicide may be explained by the fact that it was he who murdered his secretary?'

A few minutes later, Nick was on his way. Whatever anyone else might think, he was not going to be satisfied it was suicide until the pathologist had excluded every other possibility. It would therefore be necessary to advise Professor Travers that other possibilities did exist.

CHAPTER TWENTY-FIVE

Detective Chief Superintendent Rudgwick was in a bad mood by the time he got back to his station. He regarded all meetings called by his superiors at Scotland Yard as a waste of time. It was a display of blanket disapproval to which the superiors in question were resigned, fortified in the knowledge that his retirement was near. It was an attitude on Rudgwick's part which had led to his not being considered for further advancement and which had, in turn, been aggravated by knowledge of this; the vicious circle syndrome, as one of his high-flying colleagues had called it after attending a symposium which had rung with other such expressions.

He listened to Nick's account of Miles Rickard's death with a set frown and his mouth turned down in an expression of dissatisfaction.

'Why wasn't I told immediately?' he asked angrily.

'I did ask someone to phone the Yard and get a message to you, sir,' Nick replied.

'Well, I didn't get it. But what I really meant was why didn't Inspector Parkington immediately notify the C.I.D.?'

'He didn't know all the background, sir. He didn't realise the significance of Rickard's death.'

'He should have done,' Rudgwick snapped. 'There I was sitting on my backside being lectured about what the bloody computer had spewed out on criminal trends when I could have been doing something useful back here.'

Nick prudently forbore to ask what. He knew that to Rudgwick computers were no more than trendy toys which were always breaking down.

'You can stuff your clever toys,' he was always saying, 'give me more men on the beat.' The fact that no one suggested that the one was a substitute for the other made no difference.

When Nick had finished, Rudgwick said in a tone of surprising viciousness, 'Come on, we're going to pay a call on the Wenners. And if anyone thinks I'm going in for a bit of persecution, they're right.'

'Shall I let Detective Sergeant Tarry know?' Nick asked.

'No.' Rudgwick was already half way to the door and did not see Nick's faint shrug of resignation. Nick followed him out of the room, reflecting that he could always have a word with Tom Tarry later in the light of their visit.

The drive to Northwood was accomplished in silence apart from a brief and pungent discussion between Rudgwick and his driver, Harry, as to the prospects of a forthcoming Ali fight.

On this occasion they were unable to sweep up to the house as the outer gates were not only closed but firmly locked. Nick noticed, moreover, that they were fitted with a modern burglar alarm.

Twenty-five yards beyond the gates, the house had a silent, shuttered look. Rudgwick gave Nick a questioning look and then stuck his finger on the bell-push which was set into the brick pillar at the side of the gate. He kept it there for a full half-minute and was about to have a second go when a voice came through the small grille of the answering device which was immediately above the bell-push.

'There's no one 'ere,' said a rough voice.

'Open the gate,' Rudgwick snapped back.

'Shove off.'

'It's the police. Open the gate.'

'Watcher want?'

'Come on, open the gate and be quick about it.'

'I've told yer, there's no one 'ere 'cept me.'

'If you don't open this gate within a minute,' Rudgwick snarled, 'I'll get warrants to search the place under every Act that exists and one for your arrest as well.'

There was a short silence and then the voice announced, 'Stay there and I'll come.'

It was a couple of minutes before anything happened and then a figure appeared round the far side of the house. It was a man of about thirty with black curly hair and the face and figure of a beer-drinking demolition worker. Even from this distance his biceps and shoulder muscles could be seen to

152

bulge through his skin-tight crimson shirt. Beside him on a short lead walked a black Alsatian dog, turning its head to give him an expectant look every few paces.

' 'Oo d'yer want?' he asked, coming to a halt within a couple of yards of the gate. At a signal, the dog sat down.

'Where are Frank and Alec Wenner?'

'They're not 'ere.'

'Where are they?'

'Gone away.'

'Where?'

'Dunno.'

'When?'

'This morning if you 'ave to know.'

'You must know where they've gone?'

'Well, I don't.'

'What about Helen?'

'Gone, too.'

'Did they all leave together?'

' 'Sright.'

'By car?'

' 'Sright.'

'So where have they gone?'

' 'Ow many more times? I dunno.'

'When are they coming back?'

'Dunno.'

'What do you know?'

'That if you set foot inside 'ere, I'll let 'Erman 'ave a nibble at you.'

'What's your name?'

'What's yours?'

'Detective Chief Superintendent Rudgwick.'

'Thought you might be.'

'I'm still waiting to know your name.'

'Why should I tell you?'

'Because if you don't, I'll have you in a cell down at the station sooner than your pea-sized brain can send a message telling your legs to run.'

'I'm not running.'

'The time's coming when you'll wish you could. Now, what's your name?'

'Alf.'

'Alf who?'

'Alf Wilkin.'

'It'd better be Alf Wilkin or you'll be in even worse trouble.'

'I'm not in any trouble.'

'You hope! What's your connection with the Wenners?'

'I just does odd jobs for 'em sometimes.'

'Like beating people up?'

'Nuts!'

'When did you move in here?'

' 'Smorning.'

'And are you really telling me you don't know where they've gone or when they'll be back?'

' 'Sright.'

'Have they gone out of the country?'

He hesitated for a second and then gave a shrug. 'I keeps on telling yer, I dunno where they've gone.'

'Are you staying here until they get back?'

' 'Sright.'

'Where do you live when you're not doing odd jobs for the Wenners?'

'With my mum.'

'Now, isn't that touching?' Rudgwick said with a sneer, turning to Nick.

Wilkin flushed angrily. 'At least I 'ave one which some don't.'

'Don't waste your breath trying to insult me! Anyway, where does your mother live?'

'Clerkenwell.'

'It's a big district. What street, what house number?'

'Leriad Street, number eight.'

Rudgwick turned abruptly on his heel and got into his car, followed by Nick. As they drove away, they had the satisfaction of seeing Wilkin staring after the car with a worried expression.

'So Frank and Alec Wenner have done a bunk,' Rudgwick observed at large. 'I wonder where to and why?'

'Can we get a quick intercept on their phone, sir?' Nick said.

'Not quickly enough to be any use.'

154

'In that case, could we get the phone cut off so that Wilkin can't receive or make any calls?'

'That's a good idea,' Rudgwick remarked with approval. 'We'll see what we can arrange. If the Post Office won't co-operate, I've got a pair of pliers in my office.' He gave Nick one of his rare and rather sinister grins. Turning to his driver, he said, 'To the mortuary, Harry.'

There was no sign of Professor Travers' Rolls-Royce in the yard behind the mortuary where they parked. Rudgwick and Nick got out and went inside.

The mortuary attendant, who always reminded Nick of a family butcher, greeted them both affably.

'Expecting the professor within the next half hour,' he said. 'His secretary phoned a short time ago to say he'd be on his way soon.'

'I'd like to take a look at the body, Reg,' Rudgwick said.

'Certainly, Mr Rudgwick. I've got him all ready for the professor,' he added with a note of professional pride.

He led the way into the mortuary and, with a conjuror's flourish, removed the sheet which covered Miles Rickard's naked body.

'Surprising how peaceful they manage to look!' Rudgwick remarked as he stared at Rickard's face.

'Always have to have everything ready for the professor,' Reg went on, 'he doesn't like to be kept waiting.'

'Quite right, Mr Mortimer, quite right,' said a voice from the door. They turned to see Professor Travers bustling towards them, taking off his top coat and going through the motion of smoothing his hair so that all his limbs gave the impression of having been activated by the push of a button.

He hurried over to a cupboard in the corner and took out one of the surgical gowns hanging there. Over that he put on a large apron.

'So this is Miss Sharman's employer, eh?' he remarked as he walked round the corpse examining it with a concentrated gaze. 'Suicide, carbon monoxide poisoning, is that right?'

He shot this at Nick who said, 'That's what it appears to be, sir, but too many strange things have happened for us to accept suicide at face value.'

'Ah! So you'd like me to tell you whether he might have

been knocked out before he was subjected to the car fumes, is that it?' Nick nodded. 'Well, then we'd better begin with an extra careful external examination.'

Rudgwick and Nick watched as the pathologist examined Rickard's body inch by inch, starting with his feet, and giving particular attention to his head.

'Can't feel any bumps or bruises,' he said, 'but we'll have his hair off in a moment and I'll be able to take a better look. Come on, sergeant, give me a hand and we'll turn him over.'

Nick stepped forward and, averting his gaze and concentrating his mind on a green meadow he had played in as a boy, helped turn Rickard on to his front. Though he was able to control his feelings, he had never overcome his inner squeamishness in the mortuary. Many of his fellow officers were quite unmoved, but there were still a fair number like himself to whom it remained an emotional ordeal. He always suspected that there was a strong element of bravado on the part of most of those who affected no concern. The green meadow was his standby and he was always able to conjure it up in his mind's eye at such moments as this.

'No sign of any puncture marks on the skin,' Professor Travers remarked as he completed his examination of both legs and arms. A few minutes later, he was re-examining Rickard's crudely shaven head. 'No, nothing at all on the head. Let's see what we can find inside.'

It took him forty minutes to complete his autopsy. Then going over to the wash-basin, he peeled off his gloves and scrubbed his hands. While he did so, he addressed the officers over his shoulder.

'I haven't the slightest doubt that he died of carbon monoxide poisoning, consistent with the inhalation of car exhaust fumes. I can find no associated cause of death or anything to suggest other than suicide.' He seized the towel which the attendant was holding out to him and turned to face Rudgwick and Nick. With a smile, he added, 'I hope I've made your task easier, gentlemen. To a layman, it looks extremely simple. Murder, followed by the suicide of the murderer. I imagine that must be high on your list of probabilities.' He glanced at his watch. 'Great Scott! Is that the time?' He swung round to the still hovering Reg. 'Phone Westminster

156

mortuary and say I've been held up, but am now on my way.'
He thrust himself into his top-coat and made a dash for the
exit. 'Don't forget to let me know what develops,' he called
out. 'By the way, I'm going to the lab tomorrow to talk about
L.S.D. I gather they've almost completed their tests. And I've
not been idle in my researches either.'

The door closed behind him and the mortuary assumed a
post-hurricane stillness.

'It's certainly a temptingly easy solution,' Rudgwick said,
slowly.

'It's too easy, sir.'

'All we need to find out is what motive Rickard had for
murdering his secretary. Once we know that, everything'll fall
into place.'

But Nick was not persuaded. He felt that the original spark
had been lit further back, not that this necessarily disproved
the simple theory now being advanced. But as Rudgwick
himself recognised, it did depend on being able to ascertain
a motive for Miles Rickard to have murdered Eva Sharman.

'Moreover, sir,' Nick urged, 'we need to eliminate the
Wenners from our enquiry before we can accept that theory.'

'I've been thinking about the Wenners,' Rudgwick said.
'What are your plans for this evening?'

'I haven't any, sir.'

'Alas, I have, or I'd come with you.' Rudgwick's upper lip
curled in a sort of triumphant grin.

'With me, where to?'

'What's the name of the club they own?'

'The Crimson Turban.'

'That's the place. You'd better get along there and find out
what you can. Get hold of the manager, give him a shake and
see what drops out.'

'You're not suggesting I go alone, sir?'

'I'm not suggesting anything, take whom you want. Detective Sergeant Tarry might like to accompany you.'

'He was the person I had in mind, sir.'

But when Nick got home that evening and told Clare of his
plans, she became immediately thoughtful. It wasn't until he
had finished recounting the day's events that she spoke.

'I'll come, too,' she said. Holding up a hand to forestall

157

Nick's protest, she went on, 'Simon'll be back tomorrow so this is my last opportunity to be of any practical help. What's more I'll be able to tap a source which you and Tom Tarry won't have access to.' Observing Nick's mystified expression, she continued, 'Probably the best source of information in the place.'

'What are you on about, sweetheart?'

'The powder room attendant. They're always absolute mines of information. I'll bet I can get more out of the girl at the Crimson Turban than you and Tom will ever prise out of the manager.'

Nick let out a groan which seemed to reflect a combination of respect, resignation and, not least, of anxiety.

Clare, however, was aglow with cheerfulness. 'Do you realise, Nick, it'll be the first time we've been out on the town together since New Year's Eve the year before last? I must go and put on something suitable for the occasion.'

She disappeared from the room, leaving Nick to stare ruefully at his half-eaten supper. He recognised that, as so often, she was right. She could be of considerable help if she accompanied them.

When he went upstairs to change his suit and saw her in the long apple-green dress which he had always admired, he could only go across and kiss her.

'I'll need some money,' she said, helping herself to what he had just turned out of his pocket. 'Getting information from powder room ladies is a bit like playing a fruit machine.'

CHAPTER TWENTY-SIX

'It's no more than a plush clip-joint,' Tom Tarry said as they got out of the car and looked down the street to where a red neon turban was revolving over a doorway. 'The manager's a man called Louis de Marco, real name Leonard Markham born in Stoke Newington.'

'Where does he fit in with the Wenners?' Nick asked.

'Just does as he's told. As a matter of fact he's got quite a way with the customers and business has improved since he took over a couple of years ago. The previous manager looked a bit too much like a baboon.'

'What happened to him?'

'He's one of Frank Wenner's debt collectors. A pretty effective one, too.'

A doorman gave them an exaggerated salute as they arrived outside.

'Name of Felix,' Tom Tarry commented laconically. 'Not that he's ever brought anyone luck.'

'I'll leave my coat and meet you in the bar,' Clare said, heading for a door marked 'Ladies'.

In her experience, the ladies in charge of powder rooms fell into one of three categories. Artificial blonde, artificial brunette and motherly grey-haired. She guessed that the one she was about to set eyes on would belong to either the first or second category. If she was a motherly grey-haired type in a place like this, it could only mean she'd be a con woman with a strong line in soft talk.

'Good evening, madam,' said such a person as Clare came through the door. She was wearing a black satin dress with a small white apron and her grey hair was neatly waved. She wore no make-up and her whole appearance was one of quiet dignity. It was still Clare's bet, however, that she had seen the inside of a prison, and probably more than once. 'I think it's turned a little cooler this evening,' the woman added, taking Clare's coat and handing her a ticket.

Clare smiled at her and agreed. Then opening her purse, she took out a 50p piece and put it on the plate where it joined a number of 10p pieces.

'Thank you, madam, that's most kind.'

Clare gave her another smile as though it was she who had been done a favour. Her initial ground-work completed, she left to find Nick and Tom Tarry.

'What are you going to have, Clare?' Tom Tarry asked. 'It's on expenses.'

She noticed that he and Nick were both drinking whisky.

'I'd like a crême de menthe frappé,' she said.

'She always has that when someone else is paying,' Nick said quickly. 'Someone other than me, that is,' he added.

'I've heard of crême de menthe, but what's the frappé bit do to it?'

'Makes it look like a green ice flow,' Nick explained.

When the barman brought Clare's drink, Tom Tarry said, 'Is Mr de Marco in this evening?'

'I think he's in his office,' the barman replied.

'Haven't seen you before, how long have you been here?'

'I am here already two weeks.'

'What's your name?'

'Milo.'

'Where are you from?'

'I am from London.' And he moved quickly away to serve a customer at the farther end of the bar.

'A recent illegal entrant would be my guess,' Nick observed.

'Mine, too.' Tom Tarry tossed back the remainder of his drink and looked meaningly at Clare's half-full glass. 'When you're ready, Clare, I'll show you the rest of the club. Actually, there's only the dining-room to see.'

It seemed to Clare as she looked around her that the person responsible for the décor had shown an obsessive determination to keep the club's name in the mind of its clients. The shades on all the table lamps were in the shape of turbans and turban motifs adorned the walls. Over the centre of the small dance floor was suspended an enormous turban of crimson silk. In a corner of the dining-room, sat a bored-

160

looking girl wearing one, a tray of cigarettes on the table at her side.

An olive-skinned maître-d' came languorously forward as they stood in the entrance.

'You have reservations?' he enquired in a faintly insolent tone.

'No,' Tom Tarry said, 'we're on our way up to Mr de Marco's office. We'll decide later whether we want to eat.'

The maître-d' gave a small shrug and turned on his heel.

'Shall I meet you in the bar again?' Clare asked, as the men prepared to go and beard the manager.

Nick nodded. 'Take care, darling.'

A woman was just coming out of the powder room as Clare went back in. She was pleased to find it empty, which meant she wouldn't have to deploy any of her stalling tactics to get the attendant on her own.

'Hello, madam, not leaving already?' the grey-haired female remarked. 'I'm afraid things are a bit slow this evening. But I'm sure we shall be full before long.'

'Actually, I slipped out to ask you something,' Clare said with a small, conspiratorial smile. 'A friend of mine who was here a few weeks ago told me I must meet Mr Alec Wenner. Do you happen to know if he's here this evening?'

'I'm afraid you're out of luck. He won't be in this evening.'

Clare assumed a crestfallen expression.

'Oh, dear, that is disappointing. My friend said what a charming man he was and told me I must be sure to make his acquaintance.' Clare gave the woman a faintly sheepish smile. 'I gather he's very good-looking.'

The grey-haired attendant chuckled. 'He certainly has quite a reputation with the ladies.'

'Is he here most nights?'

'He usually looks in two or three nights a week. He and his father own the club, you know?'

'My friend didn't tell me that. I think he so bowled her over, she wouldn't have taken in what he did. Oh well, I shall just have to come back another evening. How long's he away for?'

'Probably not more than a few days. He and his father sometimes like to get away from London.' She lowered her voice. 'He's not only handsome, he's rich as well. They have a small hideout in Devon where no one can find them. I expect they've gone down there. Mr Alec has to escape from the ladies from time to time.'

'Doesn't he ever take one with him?' Clare asked with an exaggeratedly hopeful laugh.

'That's something I wouldn't know. Incidentally, if you do ever meet him, don't let on that I mentioned their place in Devon. Very few people know about it and it's meant to be a secret.'

'Of course I won't say anything. Actually, I'm going down to Torquay myself next weekend.'

'Their place is near Dartmoor.'

'Well, I'll look out for a rich, handsome man when I'm down there. But now I'd better be getting back to my boy-friend.' Clare opened her purse and took out another 50p piece which she dropped into the plate while giving the attendant a sly wink. 'And you'd better not tell the handsome Mr Wenner there's yet another girl anxious to meet him. It might turn his head.'

The woman chuckled again. 'More to the point I'd better not tell your boy-friend.'

Clare gave a small shriek of horror at the thought and departed, leaving the older woman still smiling to herself. She was thankful there was still a client or two who could help to relieve the tedium of her job. Most of them were stuck-up and hardly condescended to speak to her and her only redress was to listen in to their conversations when there were two or three of them together and store away anything useful in her mind. Useful, that is, to her husband who was one of the best freelance cat burglars in the job. She herself had given up crime on marrying him.

Clare went back to the bar and sat down at a table in a corner. A waiter came over but she said she would wait for her two friends who were seeing the manager on business. Milo, the barman, gave her a suspicious stare which she pretended not to notice.

It was five minutes before Nick and Tom Tarry appeared.

'Come on, Clare, we're leaving,' Nick said. 'Go and get your coat.'

Clare put on a rueful expression as she entered the powder room, her third visit in forty minutes. 'I'm afraid my boy-friend's in one of his funny moods,' she said, as she handed over the ticket for her coat. 'He wants to go on somewhere else.'

The attendant smiled indulgently and thanked Clare for yet another 50p piece. She had noticed Clare's wedding ring and was wondering whether her husband knew of his wife's carryings-on. Of course, the young slipped wedding rings on and off these days like chameleons changing colour.

'What did you find out from de Marco?' Clare asked as they walked towards the car.

'Nothing. He knows the Wenners are away, but he has no idea where. Or so he says.'

'My bet is they've slipped out of the country,' Tom Tarry said. 'They won't return until they decide the air has cleared.'

'They could be in Devon,' Clare remarked in a casual tone.

'Why Devon?'

'They've got a hideout near Dartmoor.'

It was a moment of considerable satisfaction to her when both men turned their heads simultaneously to stare at her in open-mouth surprise.

She told them of her conversation with the powder-room lady.

'I'll get through to the Devon and Cornwall police first thing in the morning,' Tom Tarry said.

'If it really is a hideout,' Nick remarked, 'they're unlikely to own it under their own name.'

'True. Anyway, there'll be no harm in having a word with the local police.'

Clare glanced at her watch. It was just after eleven o'clock. If Nick thought he was going to get away with one crème de menthe frappé, he could think again.

'I'm hungry,' she said, slipping her arm through his. 'When are we going to have something to eat?'

'Very soon now,' he replied, somewhat to her surprise as she had expected opposition. 'I just want to drop in at West End Central to pick up any messages. I told the C.I.D. duty officer that I could be contacted there.'

Tom Tarry waited in the car with Clare while Nick went

163

into the great, ugly building in Savile Row which was the headquarters of C Division.

'Funny the way Nick's and my paths crossed again,' Tarry said. 'It was the first time I'd seen him since he had that spot of trouble. It's disgusting the way anyone can make a complaint against us and immediately we become the subject of investigation. If you do your job conscientiously, it's difficult not to have a complaint made against you. What makes most of us mad is that nothing's ever done against the complainants even after enquiries have shown their allegation to be groundless. It just encourages mischief-making accusations. Try and get the D.P.P. to authorise proceedings for wasting police time and you run into a blizzard of legal evasion. It's time parliament did something. I don't mind telling you, Clare, that when you're on something like the Serious Crimes Squad complaints are showered on you like parking tickets. It's not funny.'

'I can tell *you*, Tom, that it's even less so if you're suspended from duty while the complaint's investigated.'

'I know. Poor old Nick, it must have been hell for both of you. But he seems to have bounced back all right.'

'The scars are still there to see if you know where to look.'

At that moment, Nick came hurrying out of the building.

'Can you wait a bit longer to eat?' he asked Clare as he got into the car.

'I'm obviously going to. What's happened?'

'Rickard's premises have been burned to the ground.'

CHAPTER TWENTY-SEVEN

By the time they arrived at the scene, the fire had been brought under control, but nothing had been saved.

They could see the twisted metal shapes that had a short time before been expensive motor cars, jutting above the reeking rubble of the collapsed roof and first floor. An occasional flare-up still kept the firemen active, but generally speaking it was all over.

Long before Nick and Clare reached the scene, they had been able to smell the pungent, acrid fumes which had spread to meet them.

Having driven through one of the cordons that had been set up, Nick parked behind a police car and got out. He saw a uniformed inspector he knew by sight talking to one of the fire officers and went across to them.

'Hello, sergeant,' the inspector said in a friendly voice. 'You've missed the best of it. Quite a blaze it was.'

'Luckily we were able to confine it,' the fire officer remarked. 'If the alarm had been delayed, it could easily have spread to other buildings.'

'What time did it happen?' Nick asked.

'Ten twenty-two,' the fire officer replied, used to precision in such matters. 'Still a fair number of people out and about at that hour so the alarm was raised almost immediately. Our first unit arrived here at ten thirty-one.'

'Who did raise the alarm?'

'A passer-by. He said the whole place seemed to burst into flame at once. Someone else saw a car come out of that side street like a bat out of hell and hurtle off without his lights on.'

'Those two factors make you think it's arson?'

'They most certainly do. And I'm quite sure there'll be others to confirm it when I'm able to look around inside. From the description, it sounded like a fierce, localised start to it. In other words, it was deliberately started.'

'In which case another job for the C.I.D.,' the inspector said cheerfully.

'Do you happen to know, sir, whether Detective Chief Superintendent Rudgwick has been told about the fire?'

The inspector grinned. 'I gather his response was that, provided no one was killed, he wasn't proposing to turn out. He added something about his watering can having a hole in it, anyway.'

'Of course, our first concern was to ascertain whether there was anyone trapped inside,' the fire officer went on stolidly. 'But I understand there's no one here at night. It's the sort of place I'd have expected to find a night watchman.'

'They employed one of the security organisations to make checks through the night,' Nick said. 'Mr Rickard thought it cheaper and more reliable.'

'You know the owner?'

'Knew. He committed suicide this morning.'

'That's a bit of a coincidence.'

'Believe me, nothing's a coincidence where the name of Rickard's concerned,' Nick said. Turning to the uniformed inspector, he added, 'Has anyone been in touch with the Rickard home?'

'Naturally. I sent a car round immediately I got the address. That was when I learnt about Mr Rickard's death. His stepson was at home watching television and said his mother had gone to bed and couldn't be disturbed.' Reading Nick's thoughts, he continued, 'Sergeant Pitt who went to the house was satisfied that the young man's reaction on being told of the fire was genuine. He was obviously taken completely by surprise. He said that, if it was started deliberately, you would know who was responsible. When Sergeant Pitt pressed him to be more explicit, he mentioned the name of Wenner.'

Nick nodded. 'I expect Sergeant Pitt is right, but as you already know, sir, nothing is what it seems in this case. Case! It's a never-ending string of cases.'

'There was a car parked outside the house, a Peugeot, which the young man, Upton, said was his mother's. Sergeant Pitt felt the radiator and it was quite cold. Upton told him he had used it about three hours before and not put it away in the garage as he thought the police might still want to check things there.'

Nick gave another nod. He hadn't thought it likely that Upton or his mother had set fire to the premises of Rickard Motor Distributors Limited, but he was unwilling to accept anything unless it was corroborated.

'Did anyone get a glimpse of the driver of the car that left in such a hurry when the fire started?'

'Unfortunately not. He was male, but that's about all. And worse still no one got the car number, because, as I've said, he didn't have his lights on. It was thought to be a mini.'

'Which lets out Rickard's family.'

Nick looked about him. A number of the fire appliances had already departed and the crowd of onlookers had thinned. He decided that his presence was no longer required. The necessary buttons would be pushed to try and trace the mini and its driver, but he had small hope of any success in this direction. Nor did he expect any useful clues to be found when the charred remains of Rickard's showroom were raked over.

In his own mind, he was certain that it had been the work of the Wenners. With one savage and destructive swipe they had closed their account with Rickard. Proving it, however, would be a very different matter. Even if the police were able to catch the person who had lighted the match, there was still likely to be an unspannable gap in the evidence linking him to the Wenners.

All this he expressed to Clare as they drove home, thoughts of a meal having long since been abandoned.

As he climbed into bed, he glanced at the alarm clock and groaned.

'Only five hours' sleep if I manage to drop off instantly.'

'And you're not going to go to sleep instantly,' Clare said in a determined voice. 'I've been thinking ever since the prospect of a meal faded and if you'll keep awake for ten minutes, I'll tell you just how I believe the whole thing happened.'

'The whole thing?' Nick said, sleepily snuggling down.

Clare gave him a sharp prod in the side. 'Yes, the whole thing, starting with the burglary and concluding with tonight's fire.'

167

CHAPTER TWENTY-EIGHT

In the small village on the edge of Dartmoor where the Wenners had acquired a solidly built bungalow, they were known under the name of Brown.

Not much was known about the Browns, save that they consisted of two men and one woman. Father, son and daughter-in-law was the assumption and the Wenners did nothing to rectify it.

They did not often appear at their bungalow which lay just outside the village and well hidden from prying eyes. And when they were in residence, they were seldom seen save on a quick shopping foray.

In short, they kept themselves to themselves. They didn't bother anyone and nobody bothered them. They were entitled to their privacy and their comings and goings went largely unmarked. They were town folk and though there were some who resented their intrusion, most of the village shrugged them off as harmless foreigners. Inevitably at the beginning rumours had circulated as to what they did, but these had dwindled and died through lack of nourishment. Now there was only occasional speculation about who they were and what they did.

There was therefore considerable surprise when all three of them turned up in the local pub about half past nine on what was the evening of the fire at Rickard's premises some two hundred miles away.

The son had, in fact, been in the pub before, but the father and the woman had never been within its walls and their presence aroused quite a lot of curiosity.

They sat over in a corner of the small bar drinking whisky and gins and tonic and talking amongst themselves. But they seemed to make a point of looking up and greeting new-comers, as well as anyone departing. And the younger man was affability itself whenever he came to the bar to replenish their glasses, standing the landlord and others a drink on more than one occasion.

In all, they spent about fifty minutes in the pub and when they departed they bade everyone good-night in the friendliest manner.

'We shan't be forgotten there in a hurry,' Alec Wenner said with a chuckle as he turned the car round and headed back to the bungalow.

It lay in a hollow a quarter of a mile down a narrow track and was shielded from view from the road by a copse.

Alec Wenner stopped the car outside the front door to let his father and sister get out. Then he drove round to the garage which was some twenty-five yards from the bungalow. He paused for a moment on his walk back to sniff the air. It might be sweet and healthy, but give him a bit of pollution any day. The country was too bloody still and quiet for his liking and there was absolutely nothing to do. It was all right for Frank who became more and more of an ascetic every day, and for Helen who had always quickly adjusted to every fresh facet of life, except, of course, her marriage to Miles Rickard. But he, Alec, was naturally gregarious and he missed London badly. Paris and the beaches of the Costa Brava were all right, but bloody quiet, cut-off, uncrowded Devon was not.

An owl flew silently out of the wood and caused Alec to duck suddenly as it coasted over his head. He cursed it and was glad no one had been there to see him, Alec Wenner, startled by a bird. At least, one of the other variety had never had that effect on him. And that was another deficiency in the country, no female prey. He didn't doubt that a certain amount of bouncing still took place in the hay, but that wasn't his idea of a night out. Anyway, Frank had discouraged any mixing with the locals, in particular the local girls.

'You can keep your urges bottled up when we're down there,' he had said at the outset. 'Otherwise you're likely to find yourself on the wrong end of some farmer's pitchfork.'

Alec had been obliged to agree. The whole idea of having a hideout in such a benighted area was to be able to disappear at will when occasion required. It had already proved its uses in that way. Frank had been insistent that absolutely no one should be told of its whereabouts. They could keep in touch with their affairs by telephone and there was no need for anyone to know where to call them.

If pressed, Alec would have stoutly denied having ever revealed the bungalow's existence or whereabouts to anyone, conveniently forgetting that he had hinted at its existence to a new cigarette girl at the Crimson Turban to whom he was offering a bit more than the customary freedom of his bed.

He quickened his pace and reached the bungalow. He could hear Helen moving around in the kitchen. Frank was in the living-room sitting in a hard-back chair beside the telephone.

He was holding the receiver very tight to his right ear with the other end directly in front of his mouth as though he had just been instructed how to make a call by numbers.

'Well, try again,' he said as Alec entered the room. Replacing the receiver, he looked up at his son. 'I can't get through to Alf.'

'He may have slipped out for a drink before the pubs close. I know he's not meant to, but it's a bit lonely for him in the house.'

'I don't mean he doesn't answer. The line's gone dead. I've told the girl to find out and ring me back. All she kept saying was that the line was out of order.'

Alec fluttered his hands in a gesture of well-don't-look-at-me-I-didn't-do-it.

'Telephones are always going out of order,' he said. 'Is Helen getting us something to eat? I'm hungry.'

The telephone began ringing and Frank Wenner seized it quickly, clamping the receiver to his ear. Alec watched his father's expression become a mask of anger as he listened in silence apart from an occasional grunt.

Putting the receiver back, he said, 'She now says the line appears to have been cut. The engineers will repair it as soon as they can.'

'I've heard that one before. It all depends how it got cut.'

'Exactly. If it's the police up to funny games, it'll remain cut for as long as they want. Meanwhile, we're out of touch with Alf.'

'We can ring Louis at the club.'

'What good'll that do? He can't get in touch with Alf. He won't know anything that's happened.'

'Alf may have phoned him from a call box.'

'To say what?'

'That the phone's out of order.'

'We know that. We don't need Louis to tell us what we already know.'

'He may have told Louis other things.'

'If he has, he'd better watch out for trouble next time I see him. Louis' responsibilities begin and end with managing the club.'

Alec Wenner let out a noisy sigh. 'So what do you suggest, Frank?'

'There's only one thing to do,' the older man said, giving his son a look to quail at. 'Hit back. Like we've always done.'

'Fine, but how?'

'Ask Helen to bring me a cup of black coffee and I'll tell you exactly how.'

CHAPTER TWENTY-NINE

The first thing Nick did when he arrived at the station the next morning was to find out what the fire officer had reported.

It proved to be as he had expected, namely that the fire had been deliberately started and that its point of origin appeared to be a store cupboard at the rear of the showroom which had been full of empty cartons and packing material. The inference was that these had been liberally doused with petrol and set alight. The result would have been the rapid and destructive spread of fire which had taken place. In view of the extent of the damage, it was impossible to say how the person had got into the building, but, assuming he didn't have a key, an ordinary break-in must be presumed.

Nick knew from his other enquiries that there were two main sets of keys. One held by the forecourt attendant, who was the first to arrive and who opened up the premises in the morning, and the other by Miles Rickard himself. Nick had himself authorised Rickard's set being handed to the sales manager the previous afternoon, he being next in seniority after Rickard. His reign as acting boss had, however, proved to be of short duration.

It didn't take Nick long to ascertain that both still had their keys and had not parted with them, nor used them to re-enter the premises after they had been secured around six o'clock the previous evening.

All this Nick reported to Detective Chief Superintendent Rudgwick as soon as he arrived.

'Any news of the Wenners?' Rudgwick asked in a testy voice.

Nick recounted the visit he and Sergeant Tarry had paid to The Crimson Turban, but refrained from mentioning that Clare had accompanied them.

'Who gave you the tip about their being in Devon?' Rudgwick asked.

'The cloakroom attendant, sir.'

'A he or a she?'

'A she, sir.'

'Ladies' or men's cloakroom attendant?'

'Actually, it was the ladies', sir,' Nick said in a discomfited tone.

Rudgwick nodded. 'I guessed as much. So you took your wife?'

'Yes, sir.'

'At the taxpayers' expense?'

'I wasn't proposing to claim for the one and only drink she had,' Nick said, with as much dignity as he could manage.

'That's up to you,' Rudgwick said in a suddenly off-hand tone. 'I've got to spend most of the day sitting on a board, so I'll see you when I get back this evening. I hope by then you'll have found the Wenners. I want them badly.'

Only a sadist could enjoy twisting tails the way Rudgwick did, Nick reflected as he returned to his own office. He'd twist and twist and then let go as suddenly as he had begun. It was now clear to Nick he had guessed from the outset that Clare had gone with them to the club. He had probably assumed it when he had given Nick his instructions the previous evening. It could even be the real reason why he had elected not to go himself.

By the time he reached his office, he found himself actually smiling. His telephone was ringing and he made a grab at it across his desk. It was Tom Tarry.

'I've been through to police headquarters at Exeter, Nick, and they're going to make some enquiries and call back. They thought a trio like the Wenners should be reasonably identifiable provided they ever stir from their hideout. Strangers stick out like sore thumbs once you get into the real countryside.'

'I'm going to be out most of the day, Tom, but I'll call you from time to time.'

'Where are you going to be?'

'West End and thereabouts. Moving around.'

'Tell me about it later, Nick.'

By four o'clock that afternoon, there was still no news of the Wenners' whereabouts, but Nick was feeling distinctly pleased with his own day's enquiries.

It looked as though Clare's theory of events was substantially correct.

CHAPTER THIRTY

When the telephone rang, Terry Upton jumped to answer it, as he always did, ever hopeful that he was about to be offered a part.

His mother's gaze followed him out of the room, her attention easily distracted from the television play which they had been watching.

She was still stunned by the twin events of the previous day, Miles' death and the fire. At the moment, she didn't know, and didn't want to know, what effect they were going to have on her future life.

She was still looking at the door through which her son had disappeared, trying in a half-hearted way to hear whom he was talking to when there was a faint rattle as the receiver was put back and he re-appeared. His eyes were shining with excitement.

'I've got to go out, mother. That was a producer and he thinks he has a small part for me. He got my name from Len Meyerson who told him to phone me direct as it was urgent. He wants me to meet him in a pub at Shepherd's Bush in half an hour. All right to take your car?'

'What is the play, Terry?'

'It's by a Hungarian and it's coming on at a theatre club in Fulham. The chap he'd cast for my part has suddenly dropped out. That's why he's in such a hurry to see me. He says it's a little gem of a part even if it is small.'

'Try not to be too late,' his mother said in a nervous voice.

'I should be back in just over an hour. From what Len told him I'm absolutely right for the part, but he wants to see me for himself.'

Giving his mother a quick kiss on the temple, he hurried from the room. A few seconds later she heard her car, which had remained parked outside the front door since Miles' death, accelerate down the drive.

Ronnie Jacobs, the man who had phoned Upton, had said the pub was about half way down Bella Street which wasn't far from the White City Stadium.

When he was in the vicinity, Upton studied the street map, without which his mother refused to drive a yard, and found he was almost there.

A couple of left turns and he deciphered 'Bella Street' on a sign which appeared to have weathered a number of assaults. It was a narrow, dingy street and he looked ahead for the reflected light of the pub. It must be set back, he thought, as he drove slowly down the street.

At about the half-way mark, he stopped and peered out. On his right was what appeared to be a builder's yard and on the other side a row of deserted terraced houses awaiting demolition.

Puzzled, he got out and looked around him. It was then he noticed a car parked in the entrance to the builder's yard. He was about to turn away when the driver's door opened and a man got out.

'Mr Upton?' he said.

Relief surged through Terry Upton. It must be Ronnie Jacobs. Presumably, he'd arrived to find the pub had closed down and now he was patiently waiting for Terry at the place where it had once been.

'Yes, I'm Terry Upton. You must be Mr Jacobs? I was just beginning to wonder . . .'

But he got no further for a pad of evil-smelling stuff was clamped over his nose and mouth and held there firmly despite his struggles, which were soon over. He felt his legs buckle and then the world blacked out.

When he came to, he couldn't for several moments recall what had happened, but then realisation came flooding back. With it came waves of nausea.

He was lying trussed on the floor of a car which was travelling fast. There was a gag in his mouth and he was covered by a blanket.

He managed to give a wriggle and let out a muffled sound. Almost immediately he felt the car slow down and come to a halt. It did so with a lurch and he realised it had been driven on to a verge.

176

The blanket was removed from his head and a torch was shone into his face. His eyes were still tightly shut when the beam was switched off and a voice spoke.

'So you've come round!'

Terry Upton made further noises of protest at the gag.

'O.K., I'll ungag you for a few minutes, but if you scream or shout, I'll knock you senseless. Understood?'

After receiving a muffled assent, the driver leaned over and removed the gag none too gently.

'Where am I?' Upton asked in a scared croak of a voice.

'On the floor of a car.'

'But where?'

'Somewhere in England.'

'Where are you taking me?'

'You'll find out in due course.'

It was dark outside and now that the torch had been switched off, there was complete darkness inside as well. All he could see was the outlined head and shoulders of the driver who was leaning over the front seat looking down at him.

'Please let me go,' he said. 'If you do, I promise I won't tell anyone what's happened.'

'You've a bloody nerve,' the voice said. 'You and your bloody step-father have caused enough trouble talking to the police like a couple of old washerwomen.'

'I don't know what you mean,' Upton said in an even more scared voice.

'You will soon enough.'

'What's going to happen to me?'

'That very much depends on you, mate. If you're sensible, your loved ones may see you again, though God knows why they should want to. If you're not sensible, then this could easily be your last trip.' The man bent down. 'Time to get going again. Lift up your head.' When he didn't immediately comply, he was tugged viciously by the hair, which caused him to let out a yelp. A second later his gag had been slipped back and the blanket had been rearranged to cover him. He received a final hard thump on the shoulder with an admonition to behave himself and then the engine was started and the car bumped back on to the road.

Despite acute discomfort and continuing bouts of nausea, he

must eventually have fallen asleep for the next thing he knew was that the door against which the top of his head was pressing was flung open and the blanket was whipped away. Almost immediately a blindfold was slipped over his eyes, though not before he had seen the half-light of early morning outside.

'Went without a hitch,' the driver said to someone. 'Let's get him inside and then I'll put the car away.'

The piece of rope which bound his ankles together was removed and he was hauled to his feet.

'Come on, stand up,' the driver said impatiently.

'I can't, my legs have lost their feeling,' he whimpered.

'I'll give you feeling in a moment if you don't stand up.'

Supported on either side, he was half-dragged inside a house and then with one person holding on to his shoulders and another his feet, he was lowered down a ladder like a sack of potatoes.

The blindfold and gag were removed as was the piece of cloth with which his hands were knotted behind his back.

He was in a small white-washed cell. The only light came through the square hole in the ceiling. He was aware of an older man standing there looking down. The driver of the car now scaled the ladder and the two men together pulled it up behind him.

A trap-door was lowered and Terry Upton was plunged into terrifying darkness. A few seconds later, however, a ceiling light came on and he was able to take note of his surroundings.

The only furniture was a mattress over in one corner with a blanket tossed on top of it. There was no window and the four walls were solid brick.

He staggered over to the mattress and sank down convulsed in tears of misery and fear.

Upstairs in the living-room, Frank Wenner said, 'Twenty-four hours should soften him up.'

Alec Wenner, stretched out in a chair after his long all-night drive, laughed. 'If you ask me, twenty-four minutes will do the job.'

CHAPTER THIRTY-ONE

When Pamela Rickard realised that Terry had never come home, she rang the police in a panic.

It was about eight o'clock and a soothing voice told her that Detective Sergeant Attwell would be informed as soon as he arrived.

So it was that Nick found himself for the second time in forty-eight hours paying a breakfast time visit to 'Grampians'.

He had considerable difficulty in obtaining all the details from her as, at times, she became quite incoherent. But slowly the story emerged. The phone call around half past nine; no, he never mentioned the name of the producer; yes, presumably he must have given Terry his name but Terry didn't tell her; no, nor had Terry mentioned the name of the pub where he was to meet the man, but it was near Shepherd's Bush; yes, that was as precise as she could be. He had taken her car and said he would be back in about an hour's time. She had gone to bed not long after his departure.

She kept on repeating that it was for a part in a new play by a Hungarian, as though this was a clue of considerable significance.

'What can have happened to him?' she asked in an anguished voice when Nick had finally extracted all the pieces from her.

'I'm afraid I can't tell you, Mrs Rickard, but I'm sure we'll find out something quite soon.'

'You don't think he may be dead?' she went on, anxiously searching his face for a hopeful answer.

'I've no reason to think that at all,' he replied, realising that his tone carried a singular lack of conviction.

'Why, but why are all these dreadful things happening to me?' she burst out and began to weep.

'Try and pull yourself together, Mrs Rickard. I know you've

been under a great strain, but . . .' He let the sentence trail away. He had been about to add 'but perhaps it will soon be all over.' But would it? There was a strong possibility that the strain on her would become even greater. Quickly he said, 'Have you got someone who can come in and be with you?'

'My sister lives in Manchester,' she said through tears, as though this explained everything.

'A friend, then?'

She shook her head. 'I'll be all right,' she said, dabbing her eyes. 'I'd sooner be on my own. My sister's coming tomorrow.'

When Nick returned to the station, it was not long before he learned that her abandoned car had been found in Bella Street. It was unlocked, the battery was almost run down as the parking lights had been left on and the ignition key was still in position. In answer to Nick's question, the officer at Shepherd's Bush Station told him that there was no public house in Bella Street and, so far as he was aware, there never had been.

A call to Terry Upton's agent confirmed that he had not told any producer to telephone Upton direct and that he knew nothing of any play by a Hungarian which was about to be put on at a theatre club in Fulham or anywhere else.

Nick's overall impression from the conversation was that Len Meyerson wouldn't be too concerned if his client had vanished for good.

At one stage he had said, 'Of course if he had any sort of name at all, this could be nice publicity. As it is, we can't do anything with it. Pity!'

After his call to the agent, Nick tried to get through to Tom Tarry only to find that he was out and not expected back until the early afternoon.

However, Tarry had given him the name of his contact in the Devon and Cornwall police and Nick now phoned him, only to learn that he had not received reports of anyone answering the Wenners' description. He reminded Nick that Devonshire was a large county with some remote areas and promised to ring back as soon as he had any information.

All this accomplished, Nick sat back in his office chair and stared in deep thought at the calendar which hung on the wall behind his colleague's desk. It depicted a languorous blonde reclining in a foam bath. To Nick, it lacked any trace of originality and he switched his gaze a couple of degrees to the left. At least the wall had a fresh stain to look at where a widely thrown cheese and chutney sandwich had struck.

But, in fact, Nick's concentration was on neither the blonde nor the stained wall. It was on how to interpret Terry Upton's disappearance. His immediate reaction was that the Wenners must have felt themselves in considerable danger to have made such a move, for he had no doubt that the kidnapping was their work.

Whether or not Terry Upton would be found alive was more debatable. Nick certainly had no wish to bet on it. It would probably depend on how soon the Wenners' hideout was located, for, again, Nick had little doubt that that was where he was being held.

He decided to phone Clare and tell her the latest development, which seemed to unhinge her theory. She agreed, but wondered whether it might only be an illusion.

Without understanding all the implications, she, too, felt it would be a race against time to save Terry Upton's life.

And as each hour of the day wore on without news, it seemed to Nick that the race was being lost.

'Give them twenty-four hours and they'll be in touch with *us*,' Rudgwick had said. 'That is, if we're not on to them first. There'll be demands and Upton's life will be the bargaining counter. Lay off or Upton's a goner, something of that sort.' He had let out a contemptuous snort. 'Some hope they've got.'

It was not until seven o'clock that evening that the long hoped for call from Exeter came through. It was short and to the point.

A family of three, two men and a woman, living under the name of Brown, had a bungalow outside the village of Wivelton which was about six miles from Okehampton. Their descriptions matched those of the Wenners. Moreover, they were currently in residence. What did the Met Police want doing?

The reply was equally short and to the point. The Met Police in the shape of Detective Sergeants Attwell and Tarry would be on their way within an hour.

CHAPTER THIRTY-TWO

Only a few early risers saw the three vehicles drive through Wivelton soon after six o'clock the next morning.

In the front one were two patrol officers from Okehampton. Next came Nick, Tom Tarry and a couple of C.I.D. officers from headquarters in Exeter. In the third, which was a van, there were half a dozen uniformed officers under the command of an inspector.

At a conference held around midnight when Nick and Tom Tarry had arrived from London, it had been decided to get to the bungalow before any of its occupants were likely to be up. The four C.I.D. officers would lead the raid and their uniformed colleagues would be available should reinforcements become necessary. Nick and Tom Tarry thought it most unlikely that there would be any shooting, but no chances were being taken. After the conference, Nick and Tarry dossed down in armchairs for three hours' fitful sleep.

At half past four, they were having breakfast and at five they left for the thirty miles' drive to Wivelton.

At Okehampton they picked up the patrol car, one of whose occupants had been the officer who had decided that the Browns and the Wenners could well be the same people.

'All three of them were in the local pub the evening before last. It was the first time they'd ever shown their faces like that and it caused a bit of talk in the village,' he told Nick after introductions had been made and before they set out on the final lap of their journey. 'They even bought drinks for some of the folk there.'

His description, though second-hand, left Nick in no doubt that they were, indeed, the Wenners.

'What's more,' Nick said, 'I think I can tell you why they were so determined to be noticed on that particular evening. They were giving themselves a copper-bottomed alibi for an arson job back in London.'

Twenty minutes later, Nick and the other C.I.D. officers were moving stealthily up the path which led to the bungalow. The remaining officers had been strategically posted to cut off anyone's flight.

A light shone from a window at the side of the building and Nick altered course to investigate. There was a gap in the curtains and he was able to look into the room.

What he saw made his heart give an excited skip. Lying on the floor of the room was Frank Wenner doing press-ups.

A few seconds later, the whole country seemed to reverberate with the assault that was made on the front-door, as they pummelled it with loud smacks and used its knocker like a coal hammer.

At the same time there were loud cries of, 'Police, open up.'

It was about a minute before anything happened and then they heard bolts being drawn and a key being turned and Frank Wenner stood before them.

' 'Morning, Frank,' Nick said, stepping inside. 'Glad we found you at home. Where's Upton?'

'Who?' Wenner's voice was cold.

'You know who. Terry Upton. Miles Rickard's stepson. Where is he?'

'If that's all you've come to find out, you can go away again. I've no idea where he is.'

'You had him kidnapped, didn't you?'

Frank Wenner's eyes flashed angrily. 'The Met Police have really overstepped themselves this time. I doubt whether the Commissioner will be pleased when he hears of it and you can be quite sure he's going to hear about it.'

'Quit the bluster, Frank.'

'You're not coming in without a warrant.'

'That's more like it,' Nick said, as they pushed their way past him into the hall.

At that moment, there was a commotion outside and Alec Wenner appeared in the doorway firmly held by three uniformed officers. He was tousle-headed and was wearing trousers and an anorak over his pyjamas. Like his father he was also looking extremely angry.

'We caught him getting out of a window at the back,' one

of the officers said a trifle breathlessly. 'He tried to break away from us.'

'Where's Terry Upton?' Nick asked, his face only a few inches from Wenner's.

'Don't know what you're talking about,' Alec Wenner retorted, giving his father a look which clearly asked for a lifeline.

Frank Wenner's tone was quite different when he spoke again. Gone was the truculence. Now he was the business man who felt that a deal might be possible after all.

'Let's go into the sitting-room,' he said.

'I warn you not to try anything on,' Nick remarked as they followed him.

'I'm not saying it's a fair cop, because it isn't.' Frank Wenner said with a bitter smile. 'But the fact remains you have us at a disadvantage, though not to the extent you believe. If you'd given us another day, we'd have been able to tidy up your case for you.' He gave a shrug. 'But we must take things as they are and not as we'd like them to be, your arrival here this morning having put a stopper to that.' He walked across to a desk in a corner of the room and opened a drawer from which he took out an envelope. Under the watchful and wary gaze of all the officers present, who had become even more alert when he moved, he returned to a hard, upright chair and sat down. 'I can see that you're more at ease when I'm sitting,' he observed in a faintly contemptuous tone. Taking some sheets of foolscap paper from the envelope, he looked across at Nick and said, 'This is a signed confession by the man who burgled Rickards' and who murdered the old girl. I doubt whether the police could have obtained as good a one.' He glanced from one intent face to the next. 'You were going to get it, anyway, though the circumstances of its hand-over are not exactly as I'd intended.'

He held the sheets of paper out to Nick who took them. Tom Tarry and the two Devon C.I.D. men closed in to read it at the same time as Nick. It read:

'I, Terry Upton, confess that I helped in the burglary of Rickards'. It was all my stepfather's idea as we were short of money at home and he did it to keep us going. Otherwise

184

he'd have had to sell "Grampians". My mother never knew anything about it. My stepfather said he would need my help. I didn't really want to have anything to do with it, but he said it was for my mother's sake and to save us from ruin. He told me exactly what to do and where the money was. Just in case I was seen, he said I should look like one of the clerks. He gave me a jacket like the one this clerk always wore and, being used to theatrical make-up, I was able to give myself a scar like his. I bumped into Eva Sharman as I was leaving my father's office with the money and she thought I was this clerk called Burley. Everything was fine until after the trial when various people began poking around. My stepfather realised from something Miss Sharman said that she was beginning to be suspicious and that she might put two and two together and give the whole game away. He said we were in danger and he made me put L.S.D. in her milk. He said it would be a painless death. I went to the house and did it without being seen. My stepfather became more and more depressed afterwards and that's why he committed suicide. Neither Frank nor Alec Wenner had anything at all to do with the burglary or Miss Sharman's death. I swear by Almighty God that this statement contains the truth, the whole truth and nothing but the truth. Terry Upton.'

Nick finished reading it and said nothing. Of one thing he was quite sure, the statement didn't contain the whole truth and nothing but the truth.

'Where's Upton now?' he asked in a quiet voice.

'Show them, Alec.'

Nick, Tom Tarry and one of the Devon officers followed Alec Wenner out of the living-room, across the hall and into the kitchen. The centre of the floor was covered by a bright orange fibre mat, which he pulled aside to reveal a trap-door.

'He's down there,' he said, viciously.

'Any light?' Nick asked, after the trap-door had been lifted and they found themselves gazing into darkness.

Wenner put out an arm and flicked a switch beside the kitchen door.

Immediately, there was a terrified scream below and Terry

Upton cowered on the mattress, holding an arm over his eyes.

'It's all right, it's police,' Nick said. 'I'll come down and help you up.'

With the ladder in position, Nick descended.

'Oh, thank God, you're here,' Upton said in a choked voice. He was unshaven, one eye was almost closed and there was other bruising to his face. 'I thought I was going to die. They kidnapped me and tortured me. They said they'd kill me if I didn't do exactly as they demanded. They forced me to sign a document saying I'd committed all sorts of crimes. But it's false, completely false.'

CHAPTER THIRTY-THREE

The local police station had not seen so much activity in years as when the convoy of vehicles swept into its tiny yard and the three Wenners and Terry Upton were hurried inside.

Nick didn't have much doubt that Helen Wenner would be released before the day was out. There was no evidence that she had ever been an active participant in her father's and brother's activities; or even that she had knowledge of what was going on, though she probably had some idea.

'All we've got against Frank and Alec at the moment are charges of assault,' Nick said in disgust. 'Admittedly, quite serious assaults from Upton's appearance, but that's not going to put them behind bars for long, if at all. What we lack is evidence to charge them with arson! If only we could find the chap who actually set fire to the premises, we could let him off the hook if he turned Queen's evidence.'

'Assuming it was the Wenners who put him up to it,' Tom Tarry remarked.

'I've no doubt it was.'

'Nor have I, Nick.'

'They obviously did it to teach Rickard a lesson for having put us on to them. And then they came racing down here to be out of the way when it happened, unaware that Rickard had committed suicide.'

Nick had put through a call to Rudgwick as soon as he thought he would be in his office and had reported on events. Rudgwick had given a number of satisfied grunts and told Nick to persuade the local police to allow the Met to deal with the case, even the charges arising within their local jurisdiction.

Now some two hours later, Rudgwick returned the call.

'There was a chap in a public house at Willesden last night boasting he knew something about a fire. He was in his cups

187

and confided in the barmaid. She took the number of his car when he left. It was a mini. She later told her husband who happens to be a special constable.'

'So you'll be able to trace him, sir?' Nick said eagerly.

'Will be? We have done. He's here now. Name of Donald Price. Small time operator with previous convictions like a bag of allsorts. He says that Alec Wenner gave him a couple of hundred quid to set fire to Rickard's place. Afterwards he was to phone Alf Wilkin and report how it had gone, but, surprise, surprise, the line was out of order and he couldn't get through. But as he'd been paid in advance he wasn't too depressed.'

'That's a wonderful break, sir.'

'Even C.I.D. work requires an element of luck,' Rudgwick remarked and rang off.

It was soon after this that Nick went into the room where Terry Upton was being given a meal. A doctor had attended to his injuries and, though his face still had a battered appearance, his spirits had obviously revived.

'Will you be giving me a lift back to London?' he asked.

'Yes.'

'I'd like to phone my mother and tell her I'm all right and will be home this evening. Poor old dear, she must be worried frantic.'

'You won't be going home this evening,' Nick said in a dispassionate tone.

'What do you mean?' Upton's voice shook when he spoke.

'You'll be taken back to London and charged with the murder of Eva Sharman and with the theft of £20,000. Later, you'll probably also be charged with conspiring to defeat the course of justice. The lawyers may well think up a few more charges.'

'You can't be serious. I only signed that confession because I was being tortured. It's all lies.'

Nick shook his head. 'It certainly isn't the whole truth, I grant you that. Where it departs from it is your putting all the blame on your stepfather. I don't accept that you played such an unwilling part. It seems to me you were a very active collaborator. For all I know, you may even have taken the lead part.'

'No, no! You can't say that. It's not true. You've no proof . . .'

'But I have,' Nick broke in. 'I can prove where you obtained the L.S.D. I spent yesterday making enquiries at one or two of your West End haunts. The Axiom Club. A transvestite named Felicity or Frank according to mood and time of day.' Upton's mouth gaped open and all the colour drained from his face, leaving his abrasions looking like skilful make-up. 'Yes, I thought you would recognise those names. Also you were a bit too clever over the typewriter. If your stepfather had typed that note, why weren't his fingerprints on the machine? In fact there weren't any at all. The answer was because you had wiped it clean before you put it in its case and handed it to me. Now, why should you have done that if only your stepfather's fingerprints were on it? Again the answer was you wiped it because it bore your fingerprints. It was you who typed that farewell note.'

'I didn't kill him,' Upton said, his adam's apple shuttling wildly. 'He really did commit suicide.'

'Yes, but the note he left gave the real reason and incriminated you. My guess is that you woke up and heard something untoward. You went downstairs, found what he'd done and saw the note. You destroyed it and typed a fresh one blaming the Wenners for everything.' Nick assumed a reflective expression. 'I remember the funny way you reacted when I said I was going to take possession of the typewriter. You were obviously worried. But when I was talking to your mother, you had an opportunity of wiping it clean.'

Terry Upton who had never been much of a fighter now seemed to shrivel before Nick's eyes.

Nick stood up. 'On your feet, Terry,' he said. 'You're about to get your best part yet. A starring role at the Old Bailey.'

CHAPTER THIRTY-FOUR

The mills of justice grind slowly, and are supposedly the more sure for that. Accordingly, even though Upton was now charged with the same offence of which Steve Burley had been convicted – and the police set about the task of assembling and strengthening their evidence – there was no question of an immediate pardon for Burley. Such matters take time and are given weighty consideration by the Home Office.

He was, however, immediately granted bail by the Appeal Court, pending the hearing of his appeal. Moreover, he received unofficial assurances that he was unlikely to find himself back in Wormwood Scrubs.

The day after his release, he called at the station to see Nick. Sharon Pratt was with him.

'I just wanted to say thank you,' he said in an unemotional tone. 'I gather that if it hadn't been for you, I'd probably still be inside. I'd also like to say that I realise you had to charge me on the evidence you had at the time.'

Sharon Pratt nodded her agreement with these sentiments.

'I appreciate your visit,' Nick said. 'And I'm glad everything turned out all right in the end.'

'Turned out all right in the end,' he reflected grimly. A miscarriage of justice had been rectified, but at what a cost! A murder, a suicide and arson. All these had flowed from Nick's efforts to right a wrong. Thank goodness he didn't have to present a balance sheet, for heaven knows how it would appear in terms of moral profits and losses.

Burley's voice broke in on his gloomy reflections. 'May I ask you one question? Why did you suddenly change your mind and decide I was innocent?'

Nick shrugged helplessly. 'It was the way you gave your evidence and behaved generally during the trial. I just couldn't believe you were acting the innocent. And if you weren't act-